Death of a Suitor

A Myrtle Clover Cozy Mystery, Volume 15

Elizabeth Spann Craig

Published by Elizabeth Spann Craig, 2021.

DEATH OF A SUITOR

First edition. July 27, 2021.

Written by Elizabeth Spann Craig.

Chapter One

It was 3:30 in the morning and Myrtle and Miles were drinking coffee and quietly working on their puzzles. Pasha, Myrtle's feral cat companion, was leisurely taking a bath.

Myrtle glanced over at Miles and said in something of a pointed tone, "Isn't this nice? The two of us? Quiet?"

Miles gave her a weary look. "Don't say it."

"Of course I'm going to say it. I need to point out how very nice it is to be having some quiet time together without a particular someone barging in with a bunch of foolishness."

Which was precisely the moment the doorbell rang.

Myrtle scowled.

Miles stood up to get the door and Myrtle hissed at him, "Let's not answer it."

"She'll realize we're avoiding her," said Miles in a reasonable tone.

"Maybe she'll think we nodded off doing our puzzles," suggested Myrtle.

Miles shook his head and walked over to the door as Myrtle heaved a sigh. Pasha looked up from her bath and narrowed her eyes at the door.

"We don't want her here, do we Pasha?" asked Myrtle.

Pasha swished her tail in agreement and continued staring at the door with a rather violent expression in her eyes.

Miles opened the door and a woman about sixty years old, wearing a cheerful expression stood there. "Hi all!" she said brightly.

Pasha let out a moaning growl, hair standing up on her back. Myrtle understood the feeling.

The woman gave Miles a peck on the cheek and then beamed at Myrtle. She said in a loud voice, "Are you getting your puzzle done?"

The woman, Eloise, was convinced Myrtle was deaf although Myrtle had excellent hearing. It was yet another reason to dislike Eloise, among the legions.

"Naturally," said Myrtle coolly. "Excuse me for a moment. I should feed Pasha."

Pasha did not, actually, require feeding. But Myrtle needed time away from Eloise and she suspected the black cat did, too. Although, if Pasha were to pounce on Eloise, it might make Eloise stay away.

Eloise cried out, startling Pasha, who reared her back up in response. "Oh, I forgot! I brought a present for Pasha. Let me dig it out."

Pasha watched Eloise suspiciously as she rummaged through a purse spotted with polka dots.

"Here you are," she trilled. She awkwardly held a small toy out for the cat, who regarded it disdainfully.

"I'll just put it on the floor, then," she said. "It's filled with catnip."

"Oh gosh," said Miles slowly.

"Catnip tends to enrage Pasha," said Myrtle. "The poor darling."

Sure enough, Pasha leapt on top of the cat toy, pummeling it. She ripped at the cloth with her teeth until the insides came out and there was catnip scattered all over the floor. Then Pasha rolled around in the catnip, her black fur covered in it.

Myrtle gritted her teeth.

Eloise said with a halting laugh. "Goodness. Well, I sure am sorry about that. I didn't realize cat toys had a psychological effect on Pasha."

"She's not like other cats." Myrtle realized she should try and be nice. Sometimes, it was very challenging to be nice, especially when others continued making errors in judgment. Like coming over in the middle of the night to interrupt a very nice, quiet time between friends. "Thanks for the gift, though. That was kind of you."

Miles gave her a small smile at the effort.

"I'll clean the mess up," Eloise quickly offered.

"No worries. I can manage in a little while."

Myrtle walked away to feed Pasha.

"What are y'all doing?" asked Eloise in a bright voice.

Miles cleared his throat. "We were working on puzzles, actually."

"Oh, I like doing puzzles," said Eloise cheerfully. "Where are the puzzle pieces?"

Myrtle gave a grim smile in the kitchen, rolling her eyes as she got out some canned food for Pasha.

Miles said carefully, "It's not that kind of puzzle. Myrtle was working on a crossword and I was working on a sudoku."

Eloise's voice was disappointed. "Oh. Hm. I'm not as good at those types of puzzles. I can do the puzzles where you mark what's different in one picture than the other one, though."

Miles said, "Unfortunately, that type of puzzle is on the same page as Myrtle's crossword."

Myrtle was certainly not going to sacrifice her crossword time to Eloise so that she could mark differences in two illustrations.

Eloise looked crestfallen. Then she brightened. "I know! We can watch television."

A muscle in Myrtle's temple started throbbing.

Miles said in a gentle voice, "There's not much on at this hour. There's mostly just infomercials and things."

"Myrtle?" called Eloise, who was apparently determined to ensure that something was played on the television. "Did you tape the latest *Tomorrow's Promise*?"

She had her there. Eloise knew that Myrtle taped her soap opera every day. Myrtle sighed and then said in a rather forced tone, "Yes, I have yesterday's episode. Miles and I were planning on watching it during lunch later today." The last was said in a fairly pointed manner.

"Let's watch it now! Won't that be fun? The three of us watching our favorite soap? I keep wondering if Zack and Feline are going to finally get together. I mean, they write arguments between those two, but the tension between them is electric!"

Without getting an affirmative, Eloise plopped down in Myrtle's chair, grabbed the remote, and fiddled with it until the show came up. Myrtle's teeth-gritting moved into gnashing territory.

Lest she miss any of the show, Myrtle hurried back into the room and plopped down next to Miles on the sofa. He gave her a wordless apology with his eyes and Myrtle gave him a tight smile.

Eloise yawned and maneuvered the recliner until she could put her feet up. "Yeah, I don't like this storyline as much . . . the whole Peter-can't-find-employment thing."

The Peter storyline was actually one of Myrtle's favorites. She scowled at the television, trying to listen as Eloise continued prattling on about how Zack and Feline were really soulmates and needed to spend their lives together.

Finally, unable to hear as Peter was at yet another likely ill-fated job interview, Myrtle snapped. "If you don't want to listen, Eloise, please hightail it back home."

Miles hid a smile. Eloise put her hand up to her mouth and made a zipping motion. "I'm zipping my lips," she said, unnecessarily.

Pasha, done with her food, skulked into the room again, staring fixedly at Eloise as if watching prey. Eloise did her best not to notice and stay focused on the show.

By the time the Peter scene was over with, there was a jarring, grating, gasping sound that made Myrtle jump. She saw Eloise was lying back in the recliner, mouth slack and snoring loudly.

"For heaven's sake," grouched Myrtle. She took the remote and stopped the show. She said to Miles, "You and I can watch this when we *wanted* to—today at lunch."

Miles looked over at Eloise and sighed. Myrtle said, "Come on—we're going for a walk."

"It's four o'clock in the morning," said Miles.

"Which is an absolutely fantastic time of day to go down to the dock, sit in the rockers, and look out over the lake."

Miles followed Myrtle through her backyard and down the hill to the dock. There was a boat there that Myrtle had long ago gifted to Red, but which still stayed at her dock since Red's house across the street wasn't on the water. There were two rocking chairs on the dock and Myrtle and Miles sat down. The moon was almost full and shone on the dark water. Crickets were chirping around them and there was a chorus of frogs off in the distance. Myrtle gave a happy sigh.

Miles said, "Sorry about the interruption to our puzzle time. Eloise apparently thinks she's developing a friendship with you."

Myrtle now made an *un*happy sigh. "Just because you and Eloise are going out together, that's no reason she and I need to be friends. I suspect we don't have much in common."

Miles considered this. "You both like chocolate chip cookies."

"That's hardly the basis for a relationship."

Miles said, "I agree that you don't have a lot in common. Honestly, I've not found much in common with Eloise, either."

"As I said before, she chased you and chased you and you eventually gave up. I think you ran out of steam, and you were not in love." Myrtle added, "And Pasha can't stand her."

Miles said dryly, "Well, I'll have to break up with Eloise posthaste then."

"Pasha has *excellent* judgment."

They rocked in silence for a minute or so, watching the water ripple in the light of the moon.

"Does she read?" asked Myrtle briskly, trying to find some redeeming value in the errant Eloise.

"She knows *how* to read."

"Yes, but does she read for pleasure?" asked Myrtle impatiently.

"No. That's another thing we don't have in common. I wanted her to try one of my favorite books and I genuinely think she was horrified by the suggestion."

"Was it *Absalom, Absalom!*? Because Faulkner can be tricky, you know. It might not have been the best pick for someone who doesn't have an established reading habit."

"You know I wouldn't foist Faulkner on a novice. No, I tried to interest her in *On the Beach*."

Myrtle said, "Oh, a cheerful dystopian tale. On the upside, it's short and definitely readable. I used to assign it to my high school students, so it shouldn't have been too much of a problem for her to tackle."

"That's what I thought," said Miles morosely.

They were silent again, listening as the frogs' croaks reached a crescendo.

Myrtle said, "I can add other items to the litany of things that are wrong with Eloise."

"I thought we weren't counting things that were *wrong* with Eloise. I thought we were cataloging ways she and I are different."

"Yes, but differences are things that are wrong with her. She didn't like Peter's storyline in *Tomorrow's Promise*. That was annoying."

"But she *does* watch the same show that we do, so that's technically *not* a difference," said Miles.

Myrtle said darkly, "I have the feeling she's not a longtime *Tomorrow's Promise* viewer. I mentioned the Denise Playford storyline from five years ago and she gave me the blankest look I've ever seen. Actually, she gives me that particular look quite a bit."

Miles said, "I'm not disagreeing with you. I'm simply trying to figure out the best way to handle backing out of the relationship. I don't want to hurt her feelings. And she's gone out of her way to be nice to both of us."

"By being obsequious."

"Now, Myrtle."

Myrtle said, "I know, I know. She doesn't deserve a mean breakup. There should be a fairly easy way to handle it. I'll ruminate on it. Now what are we going to do about Sleeping Beauty in there?"

"I could slip back in and bring our puzzles out here. The moon is pretty bright."

Myrtle looked leery. "That might wake her up. Then she'd want to join us on the dock."

"Actually, she wouldn't. She swore me to secrecy, but I suppose it's all right if I tell just you. Eloise can't swim and it makes her very nervous to be close to the lake."

Myrtle said, "It's very odd to live in a town with a massive lake and not sign up for swim lessons. But I'm glad you told me.

I foresee many evenings on the dock, you and I. Oh, when you go up, I have a booklight in my bedside table. I have no idea why Red gave it to me—it's not like I'm going to disturb anyone if I turn on a lamp when I can't sleep."

Miles headed back into the house and quickly came back. "She's gone."

"Gone? As in . . . disappeared?"

"Well, I don't believe she disappeared, but she definitely left." Miles looked uncomfortable. "Do you suppose she was upset when she woke up and we weren't there?"

"If she had a lick of sense, and I'm not positive she does, she'd have woken up, realized she'd fallen asleep and needed to go to bed, and left for home."

Miles said, "But what if she *didn't* have a lick of sense?"

Myrtle folded her hands in her lap. "Perhaps a masked intruder came in and spirited her away. Better her than me, of course."

Miles, at the mention of a masked intruder, had already pulled out his phone. "Eloise? Hi there. Did you make it home all right?"

There was apparently a confirmation on the other end.

Miles said, "I'm sorry Myrtle and I left. We figured having the television on might disturb you so we walked down to the dock to let you sleep."

Myrtle rolled her eyes at this fabrication on Miles's part. They'd simply wanted to escape Eloise's presence, even if she *was* sleeping.

"All right. So I'll see you tomorrow sometime? Good."

Myrtle gave him a fierce look and shook her head.

"Okay, well, sleep tight." Miles hung up.

"That's not exactly the textbook approach for breaking up with someone."

Miles said with a sigh, "I'm hoping that I'll be able to find a good method on the internet."

"I can only imagine the suggestions you'll find online. Shall we go inside and finish our puzzles?"

And so they did. And enjoyed milk and cookies while they worked them.

Chapter Two

Miles ended up going back home sometime around dawn. Myrtle dozed just a bit in her chair after he left, with Pasha curled up in her lap. Then she woke up, got ready for her day, and had a big breakfast of eggs, bacon, and fruit.

Elaine, her daughter-in-law, came by briefly before taking her son, Jack, to preschool.

"Good morning!" beamed Myrtle when she opened the door.

"Looks like you've been up for a while," said Elaine wryly. "As opposed to me."

Elaine was wearing a track suit that looked like it might have been slept in. She'd made an attempt to brush her bobbed hair, but looked like she'd missed a spot in the back, which was currently sticking straight up on the top of the back of her head.

"Just be thankful that you can sleep. You don't realize what a blessing that is. Come in and have some coffee, if you have time."

Elaine looked at her watch. "I can spare about fifteen minutes before I need to show up in the carpool line with Jack."

Elaine fixed her coffee while Myrtle visited with Jack. "Look at you!" she said to him. "You're such a big boy with your dinosaur backpack."

Jack gave her a toothy grin and then sat on her floor and carefully unpacked his backpack, showing her his show-and-tell toy, the "letter bag" full of things representing the letter *s*, and his dinosaur lunchbox.

He started playing with the box of toys that Myrtle had reserved for him as Elaine plopped down on the sofa with her coffee. "Maybe this will help me wake up a little," she mumbled. "How are things going over here?"

"Oh, they're all right, I suppose."

Elaine quirked an eyebrow. "Trouble with Miles's ladylove?"

Myrtle winced at the reference. "Eloise? Ugh, yes. Miles and I were having a completely lovely time doing puzzles last night when Eloise burst in, turned on the television, and then started loudly snoring."

Elaine hid a smile. "Really? That sounds very dramatic."

"Well, I suppose it happened in stages, but it certainly felt very sudden. Right now, I'd rather have Erma Sherman knocking on my door than Eloise."

"That really *is* bad." Elaine took another sip of coffee. "Is Miles really smitten with her, then? It seems like he's putting up with a lot."

Myrtle, who was smiling at Jack playing with toy trucks, said, "Heavens, no. No, he doesn't want to be seeing her at all. But you know how Miles doesn't like making waves. He's trying to find a way to cushion the blow when he breaks up with her. At the rate he's going, it might be next year."

Elaine leaned in as if she might somehow be overhead by someone other than a preschooler. "Okay. If that's the case, I need to share something I saw yesterday. I wasn't going to say anything if Miles was totally happy in the relationship. But I saw Eloise out yesterday with another man."

Myrtle frowned. "Out, like maybe she was stretching her legs and he was joining her? Out, like perhaps she was having a coffee and there wasn't another place to sit so this man shared her table?"

"No. Out, like they were definitely together."

"And you're sure it wasn't Miles?"

"Yes. Eloise reached out and put her hand on his and squeezed it. And then he gave her a kiss."

Myrtle said flatly, "Well, that definitely wasn't Miles. Miles doesn't believe in public displays of affection. Who was this man? Did you recognize him?"

Elaine nodded. "It was Jax Jackson."

Myrtle gave a low whistle. Jax was an attractive older man with a full beard and a rakish smile. He was tall and full of life.

"I think that's very shabby of Eloise! Imagine cheating on a kind, sweet man like Miles." Myrtle fumed.

Elaine said, "I know. Maybe break it to him gently."

"I'll do no such thing! I'm planning on giving him as much ammunition as possible so he'll actually break up with her. I'm not going to hold back," said Myrtle grimly.

Elaine glanced at her watch and took a last big gulp of coffee. "Okay, that's it for me. Hope you have a good rest of your day, Myrtle."

Myrtle gave them both hugs although she was a little absent-minded while she did so. She couldn't resist immediately letting Miles know so she gave him a call.

He must have fallen asleep because his voice was groggy when he answered. "Hmm?" he asked blearily.

"Elaine was just over here and you'll never believe what she said."

Miles said, "Jack did something cute? Or smart?"

"Of course not, Miles. That wouldn't be extraordinary at all. Jack is *always* doing something cute and smart. No, she told me that when she was out yesterday, she saw Jax Jackson and Eloise having an intimate lunch together. Kissing and handholding and whatnot."

Miles was quiet for a few moments. "Was she sure about that? Jax goes out with plenty of people. In fact, I thought he was seeing Marigold Pratt right now."

"Marigold Pratt is married."

"Yes, but that hasn't seemed to stop Jax," said Miles.

"Maybe he's seeing both of them. The point is that Elaine was absolutely certain of what and who she saw. She was planning on not saying anything because she was afraid your feelings would be hurt."

Miles said wryly, "Which is entirely the problem. My feelings *aren't* hurt."

"Precisely. And they would be if you cared about Eloise."

"My *pride* might be hurt a little, though," muttered Miles.

"Your pride should know better than to take its cues from Eloise. You have plenty of other things to be proud of."

Miles said, "It might be helpful if you were to name a few. Just to help me bounce back from this a little."

"Well, you've become much better at chess."

"That's true," said Miles. His voice brightened.

"You're very tidy. I bet most single men don't have floors that sparkle."

"I'm not sure I really feel *pride* in that, though," said Miles.

"And you're a very good friend," said Myrtle as if it had just occurred to her. "You're always very thoughtful."

"Thank you, Myrtle."

"You're welcome. Now go break up with Eloise. I know how you like to procrastinate things that you don't want to do."

Miles groaned.

"Just phone her up. She always has her phone with her. I know this because it's always going off with that annoying ringtone."

Miles said, "I don't think breaking up with someone on the phone is a very nice thing to do. And you just said that I was a good friend and very thoughtful."

"For heaven's sake! Just phone her and ask her to meet you somewhere. *She's* the one who's not valuing your relationship enough, after all. It shouldn't be that much of a hardship to cut the cord."

Miles sighed. "All right. I'll call and see if we can have breakfast together. I'll get back to you later." And he rang off.

Satisfied, Myrtle started humming to herself in a very off-key fashion while she tidied up her house. Then she finished her crossword puzzle and headed off to the grocery store for more orange juice. Red had seen to it that she didn't have a car some time ago, so when she went to the store on solo trips, she made sure that she was just getting one or two things so she could easily carry them back.

Near the grocery store, she spotted Miles and Eloise having breakfast at a table next to the window inside Bo's Diner. They appeared to be having a fabulous time together. Miles, in the middle of laughing, glanced out the window and saw Myrtle's scowling face. He quickly sobered up.

Myrtle stalked into the grocery store and found the orange juice. She also remembered she was a little low on peanut butter, so she got that as well. The bag was already going to be a bit heavy, so she stopped there and headed to the cash register.

When she passed by the diner again, Eloise was no longer there and Miles was standing glumly outside. He reached out a hand and Myrtle gave him the grocery bag.

"Did you drive here?" she asked.

"No, I walked. I wanted to clear my head."

"Did that work?" asked Myrtle.

"Not particularly."

They walked in silence for a few moments before Myrtle asked, "So what happened at the diner?"

Miles sighed. "It became very melodramatic."

"Things must have deteriorated quickly. When I was going by on my way to the store, you both looked quite jolly."

"Yes, but your expression reminded me what I was supposed to be doing. I managed an awkward segue to the subject of Jax." Miles switched the heavy grocery bag from one arm to the other. "I told her that I thought she and I needed to stop seeing each other but to continue being friends."

"Although hopefully not the type of friend that bursts into the house in the middle of the night and breaks up puzzle solving."

Miles nodded. "I think I made it clear that we weren't going to be spending a lot of time together. I didn't want to have a halfway relationship. Actually, I don't think I want to have a relationship at all right now. It certainly makes life a lot more complicated and I'm at the time of my life where I like things to be simple."

"What did she say about Jax?" asked Myrtle curiously.

"Oh, she admitted it right away. Blushed, as a matter of fact."

Myrtle said, "She couldn't have been too surprised that you found out. After all, this is a small town . . . you can't just be canoodling with someone in the middle of downtown and not have people know about it."

"Apparently, they've had an on-again, off-again relationship for a long time. Anyway, she did act rather defensive at first." Miles looked uncomfortable. "She decided to throw some of my own faults back at me. Eloise was being rather loud and I have the feeling she was overheard. It was quite crowded in the diner at the time."

Myrtle quirked her eyebrows. "What were your faults?"

"Do I really have to catalog them?"

"Well, we just listed your attributes a little while ago. It seems fair to consider your faults now, too."

Miles said, "I'm not sure they were really even faults. They were just things she didn't like—aspects of me that didn't work for her."

"Such as?"

Miles said, "Well, she thinks I'm very quiet."

"That's *definitely* not a fault and rather rude of her to say it was." Myrtle's eyes flashed.

Miles said, "Again, it was just something that she didn't care for. Eloise was always trying to get me to go out with her to a friend's get-together or a movie or to get ice cream. She didn't seem to understand my interest in puttering around the house, or doing puzzles, or reading my books."

"Non-readers are always trouble," said Myrtle darkly. "What else did she think was wrong with you?"

Miles gave her a sideways look. "That I kept odd company."

"Was she talking about me?" Myrtle was now quite indignant.

"I guess so. She could also have meant Wanda and Crazy Dan. Although I wouldn't say I keep company with them very often. But according to her, I have a real menagerie of friends."

"Hmm." Myrtle narrowed her eyes. "I believe you've had a lucky escape, Miles. A *very* lucky one. Shall we watch *Tomorrow's Promise* when we get back to my house? I can rewind it to the beginning of the show."

And so, to Myrtle's delight, the rest of the day progressed precisely as planned. They watched their show with no interruptions. They had sandwiches in the early afternoon with tomatoes that Miles had picked from his backyard garden. They sat out on Myrtle's dock for a while and listened to a mockingbird and tried to count the number of songs he was singing. It was a thoroughly delightful, unextraordinary, very quiet day. The kind of day that Eloise wouldn't have liked—which made Myrtle enjoy the day even more.

Miles left for home in the late-afternoon and Myrtle went inside to feed and visit with Pasha. She picked up her book to read when there was a knock at her door. She frowned—it was ten o'clock at night. Opening the door, she saw Miles there, a worried look on his face.

"Goodness, Miles. Has something happened?"

Miles said grimly, "Eloise just called me."

"Does she not understand how breakups work?"

"Oh, she does. But she said that Jax Jackson was dead. She found him a few minutes ago."

Chapter Three

Myrtle said, "Let's get over there."

"I think she's already called Red," said Miles.

"Maybe we can beat him there. At this hour, he's probably already in the bed. It'll take him a minute to get his uniform on."

Sure enough, as Miles drove Myrtle away, Red's police cruiser was still in his driveway.

Miles said as he drove, "She sounded pretty upset. I think she called me totally reflexively."

"It's just as well you broke up with her, Miles. Because why was she over at Jax's house to begin with?"

They pulled up to a brick ranch-style house that was on the lake. Eloise was sitting on Jax's front steps, her head in her hands. She jumped up and hurried over as soon as she saw them arrive. When Miles stepped out of the car, she threw her arms around him while Myrtle watched through narrowed eyes.

"I knew you would come, Miles! Oh, it was *awful*. Just terrible. Jax was always so full of life and there he was, lying on the floor, no life at all in him." Eloise burst into tears.

Myrtle, never a fan of tears, hastily rummaged in her huge purse for a pack of tissues which she thrust at Eloise. "Was his door unlocked?" she asked.

Eloise took a tissue and blew her nose. "Umm . . . yes, I think so. Yes, it must have been because I don't have a key and I wouldn't have been able to get in, otherwise."

Before Myrtle could ask more questions, Red pulled up, his lights going. Myrtle gave an exasperated sigh.

Red jumped out and hurried over. "You okay?" he asked Eloise and she nodded, still sniffing. He turned to Myrtle. "Mama, somehow I'm not too surprised to see you out here."

"Eloise called Miles," said Myrtle with a shrug.

Red turned to go in the house, fishing his phone out of his pocket as he went.

"He'll be calling the state police," said Myrtle. "I do hope it's Lieutenant Perkins that they send over." She turned to Eloise. "Now tell me exactly what you saw."

Eloise said sadly, "Well, I was going over to see Jax. Just a short visit, you know. He's sort of a night owl and I couldn't sleep because I have a sort of messed-up schedule." Her eyes flashed and she gave Myrtle and Miles disapproving looks as if they were completely responsible for her lack of sleep. Myrtle regarded her coolly.

"I understand that you and Jax are . . . friends?" asked Myrtle.

Miles looked miserably at the ground.

"Well, I suppose we're a bit more than that." Eloise had the grace to blush. "Although we don't always get along perfectly. Does anyone?"

"Why didn't you sometimes get along?" asked Myrtle quickly. She was trying to fit in as many questions as she possibly could before Red came over and ruined everything.

"Oh, you know. Jax annoyed me because he didn't like my baby."

Myrtle looked blankly at her. "Your grandbaby?"

"No, my little dog, Bingo. You've met Bingo, haven't you, Myrtle?"

"I've only seen pictures," said Myrtle crisply. "So he wasn't a fan of your dog. Was there anything else?"

"Not really. I mean, Jax was mostly fun to hang out with. He loved going out. Not everyone does." She gave Miles a reproachful look and Miles sighed and looked at his car, clearly wanting to be back in it as soon as possible.

"It sounds as if he was out quite a lot. You and he were spotted having lunch together." Myrtle's voice was pointed.

Eloise blushed again. "I suppose we were. But that's the way Jax *was*. He loved going to the movies or out to eat. He didn't want to go by himself—why would he?"

Myrtle wasn't about to join the Poor Jax club. She suspected that Jax had gotten himself into quite a pickle by seeing too many women at the same time. "Who else did he like to go out with?" she asked.

"Marigold," answered Eloise shortly.

Myrtle frowned at this second mention of married Marigold seeing someone. "Marigold? She's married to Bailey Pratt, isn't she?"

Eloise gave the trilling laugh that always managed to set Myrtle's teeth on edge. "Oh, Myrtle. You're really from a different era, aren't you?"

"An era that made a lot more sense."

"Everyone knows about them. Marigold and Jax have been seeing each other for quite some time."

Myrtle glanced at Miles and he shrugged. Apparently, he knew, too.

"And Bailey Pratt? Does he know about his wife seeing Jax?" asked Myrtle.

"If he doesn't, he's the only person in town."

Myrtle saw that Red was wrapping up his phone call and seized the moment, orchestrating a dizzying change of subject. "Where were you earlier this evening?"

Eloise blinked at her. "You think I had something to do with Jax's death?"

Myrtle just waited. Eloise said, "Well, I was on the phone with Miles. Miles, you remember that."

Miles said slowly, "We were on the phone together, yes. Although I doubt a phone call precludes you from homicide."

And on that note, Red came over to speak with Eloise. But first, he dismissed Myrtle and Miles. "Y'all are just going to be in the way once all the state cops get here. And it doesn't sound as if you know anything."

Myrtle bristled at that, but before she could make a retort, Red gave Miles a considering look. "I do believe I'm going to need to chat with you later on today, though, Miles. I'll be in touch."

Myrtle was grumbling as she and Miles got back into the car. "I don't know why Red needs to talk to *you*. It's not as if you know anything that I don't know."

Miles gave another sigh. "It's because he thinks I'm a suspect."

"What? He wouldn't. Red is many things, but he's not stupid."

"It's his job, Myrtle. He has to consider all the options. And, let's face it, I'm definitely an option."

Myrtle glowered out the window at the darkness they were driving through. "That's completely absurd and a waste of police time. You've been with me practically all the time."

"We don't know exactly when Jax was murdered but I don't believe you're going to be able to give me an iron-clad alibi," said Miles in his steady voice. "Think about it. I could have been enraged that Jax was seeing Eloise and stealing her away from me."

"But you *weren't*. You were trying to break up with that woman! Oh, this is all that Eloise's fault. I swear she engineered the whole thing. Maybe getting you taken off to jail is her revenge for your dumping her."

Miles gave her a sideways look before looking back at the road. "I hardly think that's the case. Red is at least considering the possibility that I killed Jax in a jealous rage. You said Elaine was the one who told you that Jax and Eloise were out together—she probably told Red, too."

"This is all most aggravating." Myrtle folded her arms. "Now I'm all keyed up."

Miles said, "You need to get unkeyed. Remember, you have a big day tomorrow."

Myrtle frowned at him and then her eyes widened. "Book club at my house! This whole mess with Eloise has made me lose my mind."

"You really don't have anything to do to prepare for it, you know. The house looks fine and we'll all just pull your kitchen chairs into the living room."

Myrtle said, "But there are snacks to get! Food to prepare."

Miles quickly interjected, "No, no. Remember, book club recently changed the rules. If you're hosting, that's *all* you're responsible for. So you don't have to provide refreshments."

"It seems rather ungracious for a hostess to require guests to bring their own food." Myrtle's brow furrowed some more.

"But it's what the club decided," said Miles with an air of finality. "If you prepare food, you'll have far too many snacks on hand."

"It's still a very odd set-up," grumbled Myrtle. "Who on earth even came up with that?"

"It was decided last month. By Tippy." Miles carefully didn't remind Myrtle that the rule was born directly after everyone realized Myrtle would be the hostess for the next meeting. He maneuvered the subject into safer waters. "Do you think everyone has read the book?"

"They certainly should have. I picked an easy title on purpose. There are no excuses this time."

Miles smiled. "I'm not sure everyone would think *Ethan Frome* an easy read."

"Then that's their own fault and a sign of their cognitive decline. I taught high school students that book, for heaven's sake. And Edith Wharton is always a delight to read." Myrtle sniffed.

"It's not a very *happy* book, though, is it?" mused Miles. "Ethan had quite the life."

"All good books don't have to be happy books. Look at Dickens. He absolutely tortured his characters with ghosts and hunger and crime and all sorts of things, but we all love Dickens." Myrtle sighed. "I hope Puddin does a good job cleaning tomorrow morning. I asked her to come a week ago. We'll see if she actually shows up."

Puddin was Myrtle's housekeeper. She had a very casual attitude toward work and was fond of taking lots of breaks. She also liked using Myrtle's cleaning supplies instead of bringing her own.

Miles pulled into Myrtle's driveway. "No one will even notice if it's a little dusty in there. They'll all be trying to figure out something to say about *Ethan Frome* to prove they actually read it. There's nothing like sitting under the eye of a former English teacher."

"Well, *I'll* notice. The dust will distract me during the entire time. I'll just have to keep a close eye on Puddin tomorrow."

Miles waited for Myrtle to get out of the car. She paused. "Why don't you come inside? I'm totally serious about being keyed up. There's no way I'll be able to sleep right now and I doubt you will, either. We've both had a very trying day."

Miles looked at his watch. "I suppose I could come in for a little while."

"I'll make us some warm milk. That's something my mother always used to do to help me sleep."

Miles made a face. "I'll turn down the warm milk."

"All right then...how about warm cocoa? It's just warm milk with chocolate mix in it."

So it was decided. The two went inside in search of boring things to do that would settle them down while they drank cocoa.

Myrtle brought out two decks of cards and they played solitaire next to each other. They'd decided that two-player games might be too exciting and would defeat the purpose. It was while Myrtle had just found an ace to put at the top of her stacks and Miles had just won his game that there was a knock on the door. They both froze, looking at each other.

Miles looked anxious. "Maybe it's Red, wanting to have that talk with me."

"As long as it's not Eloise," said Myrtle. "I'll send her off with a flea in her ear."

But it wasn't Eloise. It was Marigold Pratt. Ordinarily, Marigold was immaculately dressed in bright colors that contrasted with her snowy white hair. She usually wore coordinating jewelry. Now, however, she looked stressed, wore not a bit of makeup, and was in a tracksuit. Myrtle blinked at the apparition before her as if not quite sure it was Marigold at all.

"Hi, Myrtle," said Marigold breathily as if she'd run all the way there. "I was hoping I'd find you awake. Can I please come inside?"

"Of course," said Myrtle, stepping to the side and allowing Marigold to come in. Marigold looked flustered as she spotted Miles looking up from his solitaire game. "Goodness. You have company and everything."

Myrtle waved this statement away. "It's just Miles. Have a seat. We were playing cards."

"What game?" asked Marigold, looking a little listless.

"Solitaire," said Myrtle as if that was a common group endeavor. "What can I do for you?" Myrtle was in no mood for any foolishness, not while she was trying to wind down from a busy day. It was time for Marigold to get straight to the point.

Marigold swallowed. "Well, I know it's terribly wrong, but Jax and I have been seeing each other. I called him just a little bit ago and Red answered. He said Jax was dead."

"Hopefully he wasn't quite that blunt about it," said Myrtle.

"No, he wasn't. He sounded kind, but busy. He wasn't going to give me any information at all and acted like he needed to get off the phone. But then I started to get a call coming in, so I got off the phone with Red and answered it. It was Eloise." Marigold's face darkened.

Myrtle and Miles glanced at each other. It seemed odd that Eloise would call Marigold, of all people. Wasn't it Marigold that Eloise was upset about?

Marigold said, "I know what you're thinking. At least, I believe I do. You probably know that Eloise was seeing Jax, too."

"Some of us were the last to know," said Miles gloomily.

Marigold blushed. "Oh dear. Yes, I'd forgotten you two were in a relationship. What a mess this all is. Anyway, I can tell you exactly why Eloise called me—she wanted to rub it in that Jax was dead. She wanted to be the one who was plunging that knife in my heart. Metaphorically speaking, of course."

Myrtle said, "So Eloise called you to rub it in that Jax had died."

"And to feel a little superior—that she knew something that I didn't. But I'd already heard, of course, so her upper hand was effectively destroyed." Satisfaction rang in Marigold's voice.

Myrtle asked, "How long had you and Jax been seeing each other?"

"It's been a while. Maybe almost a year?" Marigold rubbed her forehead and looked tired. "Bailey travels a lot for his sales job and that had given Jax and me plenty of time to see each other."

Miles seemed sort of unsettled by all this blatant infidelity. "And Bailey was aware of this arrangement? Or was it a secret?"

Marigold sighed. "If he doesn't know, it's because he's determined *not* to. Bailey's big love is his job. I think he just carefully looked the other way. Plus, he's gone most of the time, so maybe he didn't have the opportunity to really see what was happening."

"Is he home now?"

"He is. He's asleep, though. He flew in this afternoon and we had a nice supper together, watched a little TV, then he fell asleep. That's when I called Jax and found out from Red that Jax was . . . gone." A tear pooled up in one of Marigold's eyes and Myrtle watched it with apprehension.

Just to be on the safe side, Myrtle batted a box of tissues closer to Marigold. "So you were at home with Bailey when Jax was murdered."

"He *was* murdered then? I figured he must have been since Red was there. Tell me what you know." It was more of a demand than a question.

Myrtle shook her head. "I don't really know anything, Marigold. Red's not exactly in the habit of sharing information with me about his cases. All I know is that Eloise discovered him, called Miles, and we went over there. But the fact that Red called in the state police means that he believed Jax to have died in unusual circumstances."

"And Eloise didn't give you any information about what she'd seen? I didn't want to give her the pleasure of telling me about it."

Myrtle frowned. "As a matter of fact, she *didn't* tell us what she'd seen." She turned to Miles, who shrugged. "Well, that was very sloppy of us, Miles! Usually we get more information than that. We became distracted by the whole Eloise-seeing-Jax part of it. For heaven's sake." She paused thoughtfully. "We could give Eloise a call."

Chapter Four

Marigold raised an eyebrow. "Well, I'm certainly not calling her."

Miles hurriedly said, "Don't look at me. I'm trying to keep my distance."

"Then I shall do it myself. Which is always the way to do things if you want them done right, anyway." Myrtle pulled out her cell phone and peered at her contacts list.

Miles said, "Don't you think she might have turned in by now?"

"I don't. She just had quite a disturbing experience. She might be in bed, but I know she's not sleeping."

Sure enough, Eloise answered the phone with alacrity, sounding fully awake and alert. "Myrtle? Is everything okay?"

"It's just fine, Eloise. But I realized just a minute ago that you never talked about what *happened* to Jax. You mentioned that you'd gone over there for a late visit and spoke about your relationship with him. But you didn't talk about a cause of death."

Eloise said, "Didn't I?" She hesitated. "Red told me not to tell anyone what I'd seen."

Myrtle walked out of earshot of the others. "I'm the only one you should tell. But don't say a word to anyone else."

"I suppose it's all right since you're Red's mother. Anyway, it was the weirdest thing. He was covered by some sort of beverage—it was all over him."

"A beverage? What, like a glass of water?"

"It was probably coffee or tea because there was a mug nearby. And he was slumped on the floor right next to his kitchen counter."

Myrtle said, "But this doesn't sound like foul play at all, does it? It sounds like he had a heart attack, convulsed, spilled his coffee or tea or whatever, and then fell to the floor. It's unlikely that Red would have called in the state police if it hadn't been a suspicious death, though."

"There was blood on the floor, around his head. Maybe that's why?"

Myrtle said, "What kind of counter does he have? You said he was by the counter."

"It's granite."

"Hmm," Myrtle said. "Maybe he hit his head on the way down." Now eager to get off the phone as quickly as possible, she added, "Well, thanks for this, Eloise. You know how curious I can be and I wasn't sure I could sleep tonight if I kept mulling this over."

"I thought you didn't sleep *most* nights."

"True. But I like to improve the odds. Thanks."

Myrtle hung up the phone and walked back over to join the others. "She didn't know what had happened, unfortunately," lied Myrtle.

Marigold said, "Are we *sure* Jax was murdered? It just seems so unlikely to me. Couldn't his death have been from natural causes?"

"I seriously doubt it. And the only reason I can say that with confidence is because Red called the state police."

Marigold stood up. "Thanks for making the call, Myrtle. Now I've just got to try to make myself believe that Jax is really gone."

Myrtle wasn't quite ready for Marigold to leave yet. "I was wondering something myself, Marigold."

Marigold sat back down and looked warily at Myrtle. "Wondering about what?"

"Since it seems Jax *was* murdered, who do you think might possibly be responsible?"

Marigold considered this. She sighed. "I suppose his daughter, Nicole, but she always sort of gets on my nerves, so perhaps I'm just being ungracious."

Myrtle said, "I don't think I know Nicole. What's she like?"

"Not at all friendly to me," said Marigold dryly. "It made me wonder if Nicole was worried that I was going to divorce Bailey and marry Jax."

"Was that something you were considering?" asked Myrtle, raising her eyebrows.

Marigold nodded. "It wasn't outside the realm of possibility. I kept reminding myself that the grass was always greener on the other side of the fence. But I don't exactly feel close to Bailey and had been sharing more of my life and time with Jax. Anyway, Nicole seems like she is always living above her means or *wants* to live above them."

"Big house? Expensive car?" asked Myrtle with curiosity.

"More like fancy vacations and designer clothes and purses. She's always really flamboyant and dramatic, too, as if she's on stage the whole time. I don't feel like I really know her. And she hovered a lot around Jax. She was always popping in to see him and she didn't leave when I was there. I could tell by the look on her face that she disapproved."

Miles said, "Maybe she was the kind of daughter who was always going to disapprove, no matter who Jax was seeing. Is she just really overprotective?"

Marigold snorted. "That's nice of you to say, Miles, but I'm afraid it's not true. Well, it's not true that she was overprotective of *Jax*. But she was definitely overprotective of Jax's money. That's the impression she gives, anyway. And I don't think she likes me one jot. It was driving me crazy. I'd plead with Jax not to answer the door but he'd always let her in."

Myrtle said, "I'd never gotten the impression that Jax had a lot of money. Or that he cared about it all that much. Didn't he drive an older model car?"

"Oh, yes. Jax liked to spend money, but on things that gave him pleasure, and those were always the little things. Concerts, movies, hotdogs over at Bo's Diner. He was a happy-go-lucky man. My happiest times with him were when we'd just hang out on his back porch, listen to music, and we'd eat lunch and laugh. Good times."

Marigold looked perilously close to tears again, so Myrtle quickly interjected, "But the money? You said Nicole is interested in his money. That implies that he had more than just a little money to play around with."

Marigold nodded and got a conspiratorial look on her face. She leaned forward as if someone might somehow overhear them in Myrtle's living room. "Well, that's something of interest. I'm sure Red will find out at some point. Jax had lived on that three-acre property of his for ages, you know. A real estate developer wants to put an apartment complex there. It would have meant big money for Jax . . . quite a payout, from what I understand."

Miles nodded. "But Jax didn't want to sell it."

"He sure didn't, no matter how Nicole tried to persuade him. Like I said, he and I were happy to sit on his back porch and look at the water. He wouldn't have traded that view for a million dollars."

"*Would* it have been a million dollars?" asked Myrtle, brows raised.

"Oh yes. It was going to be more, I believe. They kept increasing the amount of their offer after Jax continued turning them down."

Myrtle said, "He sounds like he was being very sensible to me. When you're happy somewhere, you shouldn't mess that up by moving. Nicole had a very good motive, it seems."

Marigold said, "I certainly think so. I wouldn't mind that young miss being taken down a peg or two. I'm not saying I want her arrested, mind you, but I sure wouldn't mind if Red put a little fear into her heart."

"I'm not sure that Red's interviews are ever all that frightening," said Myrtle. "But they might be if you were guilty and thought that you might go to prison."

"Exactly." Marigold looked at the rooster clock visible on Myrtle's kitchen wall. "I should get out of your hair now, Myrtle. Sorry to disturb you two, but thanks for the information."

Myrtle let her out and then closed and locked the door behind her.

Miles said, "Why do I have the feeling that you got more information from Eloise than you let on?"

"Jax apparently was covered by whatever he was drinking . . . Eloise thought it was tea or coffee."

Miles said slowly, "But if you were drinking tea or coffee and you *did* have a medical emergency, it doesn't seem likely that you'd be *covered* in it, does it? I mean, was it on his face, too? Or just dribbled down his front?"

Myrtle looked thoughtful. "Good point. Maybe that's what Red noticed. If he had his drink all over his face, it would seem like someone possibly threw it at him. Maybe that's what made him think it could be murder." After a pause, Myrtle added, "This is all very interesting."

"Which part of it?" asked Miles.

"A couple of parts. First off, Eloise and Marigold's relationship."

Miles said, "It doesn't sound like there really is one."

"Precisely. Those two actively dislike each other and it seems to revolve around Jax. I wonder if Jax was the type of man who enjoyed playing people off of each other."

Miles shrugged. "He sounds like the kind of man who really just wanted to do whatever he wanted to do. Maybe he was a mite selfish. He certainly didn't worry about seeing a married woman and breaking up a marriage. Nor seeing someone who was in a relationship with someone else."

"Now, there's no reason to be bitter, Miles. Remember, you didn't want Eloise to begin with. Anyway, that's one of the interesting things I got from our conversation with Marigold. The other one is that Nicole sounds like a real piece of work."

"Either that or Marigold just didn't like Jax's daughter very much."

Myrtle said, "It sounded like Marigold didn't like Nicole because Nicole didn't like *her*. Anyway, it does make sense if Nicole is a big spender and wants Jax's property to sell to the developer. Imagine what she could do with a million dollars or more? What would *you* do with that kind of money, Miles?"

Miles shifted in his chair as if the thought of that kind of money made him distinctly uncomfortable. "Well, I suppose I would invest it," he said stiffly.

"That sounds like lots of fun, Miles."

Miles shrugged. "I might give some of it away. Wanda could certainly use it."

Wanda was Miles's cousin and lived in a hubcap-covered shack with her brother, Crazy Dan. She was also psychic and wrote a horoscope column for the newspaper that was quite popular.

"That's very generous of you. Wanda would indeed be a worthy recipient. Of course, Crazy Dan is your cousin, as well."

Miles made a face. "I don't see myself giving Dan any money. We know he has that hoarding tendency. He'd end up buying things online and stowing them in stacks." He paused. "What would you do with that kind of money, Myrtle?"

Myrtle said with a smile, "I might set up my own detective agency. Wouldn't that be fun? Aside from that, though, there really isn't anything I need."

"Travel?" broached Miles.

"I do enjoy traveling, but the last couple of times I did it, things could get annoying. I think I've become a bit more of a homebody."

Miles yawned. "Speaking of homebodies, I should be heading back to my own abode. I think I'm feeling sleepy. Aren't you?"

Myrtle sighed. "I don't know. That visit with Marigold sort of livened me up again. Maybe I'll try and lie down for a while and see what happens. Want to come by tomorrow and have breakfast with me?"

Breakfast was ordinarily a safe meal to have with Myrtle. Myrtle's cooking, at any other time of the day, was something to be feared and avoided at all costs.

"Sure," said Miles. "Should we play it safe and make it for slightly later? In case we sleep in?"

"Okay," said Myrtle. "Six-thirty?"

"If you *sleep in*?"

"You'll have to check my pulse if I sleep past six. You know that, Miles," said Myrtle impatiently.

"Well, I believe that I might sleep just a bit later than that, after all the excitement. Let's make it eight o'clock."

Myrtle grumbled, "I might be on a second or third breakfast by then."

Miles did make it over at eight o'clock and Myrtle gave every evidence of having been awake for quite some time. She'd made fluffy pancakes, scrambled eggs, bacon, and set out some local jam to have with toast.

"This is a feast," said Miles. He wondered again how Myrtle had been able to master breakfast so successfully, considering her culinary shortfalls at other times of the day.

"I haven't eaten yet," said Myrtle. "I decided to just drink coffee. But now the coffee has been sloshing around in my stomach for a few hours and I need something to soak it all up."

They sat at the kitchen table together. Miles had his sudoku from home and Myrtle was working from her crossword puzzle book since she'd already worked the puzzle in the morning paper. They ate in happy silence for a while. Until there was a knock at the door.

"For heaven's sake! It's like Grand Central Station here." Myrtle got up and stalked to the door, peering out the window. "It's Red."

Miles carefully put his fork down. "Uh-oh."

"I'm sure he's here to see me. He's probably found out about that visit I had to Greener Pastures Retirement Home the other day." Myrtle appeared in no hurry to let Red inside.

"Did you spur another insurrection?" asked Miles.

"Only a minor one. I reminded the poor inmates that they weren't prisoners over there. They could leave. And they could protest conditions. They had a small parade of cars that went around and around the parking lot with signs for better food."

Red knocked again, this time a bit louder and harder.

"And how did the parade go?" Miles hid a smile. The insurrections at Greener Pastures never seemed to go exactly as Myrtle imagined them.

"They made quite the impression on the staff, I heard. Until there was a fender-bender."

"Hmm."

The doorbell rang several times in a row.

"You'd think Red would have even worse blood pressure than he does," mused Myrtle. "He gets so excitable sometimes."

"Perhaps you should let him inside," suggested Miles. "I don't fancy the idea of having an angry Red interviewing me."

Myrtle finally opened the door. Her son was standing there on the doorstep, quite flushed in the face.

Chapter Five

"Temper, temper," she said, making a tsking sound.

"Mama. What took you so long? I was starting to think I was going to have to break in. You might have been lying on the floor with a broken hip or something."

"What a ridiculous idea! I'm very sure-footed, Red. You know that. Besides, Miles is here."

Miles raised a hand in greeting and swallowed.

Red nodded his head. "Hi there, Miles. Sorry you're having to put up with Mama's nonsense so early in the day. I was hoping I'd see you here. I ran by your house and didn't get any answer."

Miles gave a hoarse chuckle. "Yes, well, your mom made a nice breakfast for me."

Red looked at the remains of the breakfast skeptically. "If you say so. I'm glad I found you. I thought you might have skipped out of town." He grinned at Miles.

Miles shifted in his chair. "Did you need to ask me some questions?"

"I'm afraid I do. It's just the nature of the job, you know." He turned to Myrtle. "Do you have any coffee left, Mama?"

Myrtle put her hands on her hips. "I'm not sure if I want to offer you any hospitality if you're going to be mean to Miles."

Red's eyebrows flew up. "Mean to Miles? Mama, I'm just asking him a few basic questions."

"Maybe we want Lieutenant Perkins to ask them." Myrtle put her chin in the air.

Miles apparently didn't want to be involved in this contretemps. "Myrtle, it's fine if Red wants to ask me questions. I don't have a problem with that."

"Thank you, Miles." Red went in search of his own coffee, which he poured black. He sat down across from Miles. "Now I hear that you were involved in some sort of love triangle."

Miles's face went pale and then bright-red. "Oh no. Is that what people are saying around town?"

"I don't think that's what *people* are saying, necessarily. It's just what I've picked up from other people involved in this investigation."

Miles said miserably, "Well, it sure won't take long for it to spread around town, that's for sure. I had no idea that I was involved in a love triangle, actually, until right before Jax's death."

Myrtle exclaimed, "Miles! You shouldn't say things like that."

"It's the truth, though."

"Maybe you should have a lawyer present," said Myrtle, glaring at Red.

Red raised his hands in surrender. "If Miles wants a lawyer here, then by all means."

Miles said coldly, "I don't *need* a lawyer. I had nothing to do with Jax's death. As a matter of fact, I was trying to extricate myself from my relationship with Eloise. Finding out that Jax had been seeing Eloise provided an excellent excuse."

Myrtle interjected, "He was *delighted* that Jax was dating Eloise. He was practically walking on air."

Red looked doubtfully at Miles, unable to picture that sort of effervescence in conjunction with the somber man in front of him. "Okay. So you and Eloise were dating. But you weren't completely happy in the relationship."

"Who would be?" muttered Myrtle.

Red continued, ignoring his mother. "You were looking for a way out. And you learned that Jax and Eloise were seeing each other."

"Elaine told me about it," said Myrtle. "Although you probably know that."

Red looked sorry that his wife's name was being dragged into a murder investigation, even tangentially. "And you told Miles."

"Of course I did. It was exactly the kind of information that was going to help extricate him from that relationship."

Red turned back to Miles. "And then you broke up with Eloise?"

"I did. As best I could," said Miles.

"But Eloise called you," said Red.

Myrtle said in a sour voice, "We suspect that Eloise doesn't completely understand how break-ups actually work."

"She told you about Jax's death," continued Red.

"Miles was with me the whole time," said Myrtle immediately.

Miles looked at Myrtle with wide eyes.

Red frowned. "The whole time? You mean there was no opportunity for Miles to have seen Jax?"

"Absolutely none."

Red tilted his head to one side. "That seems like a rather long time for a visit. What were you doing over here that whole time?"

Myrtle looked down her nose at him. "A variety of high-minded and intellectual pursuits. We played chess for a while. Then we played cards. We worked on our puzzles and discussed *Ethan Frome*, which is our book club selection for the meeting today. And then we relaxed by watching television."

"*Tomorrow's Promise*, I presume." Red's eyes had something of a teasing light in them which made Miles blush.

"A busy mind needs a break every now and then," said Myrtle with a sniff.

Red gave Miles a thoughtful look before getting up. "Okay. Well, thanks for the information, Miles. Hope everything goes well at garden club today."

"*Book* club," said Myrtle shortly as she followed Red to the door and carefully closed and locked it behind him.

Miles said solemnly, "Myrtle, you lied."

"I gave you an alibi. Think about it, Miles—the police would be completely wasting their time if they started wholeheartedly investigating you. It would be totally counter-productive. You had nothing to do with Jax's death."

Miles said, "I just hope no one wrecks your alibi. Then we'd both get into trouble."

"No one would dare," said Myrtle, her eyes narrowing. It boded ill for anyone who even considered it. "And I just can't tell you how very annoyed I am with Red."

"You're *always* annoyed with Red."

"Especially right now." She picked up her phone and carefully dialed her yard man, Dusty.

Dusty answered the phone sounding groggy and defensive. "H'lo?"

"Dusty. It's Myrtle Clover."

"Too wet to mow, Miz Clover!" howled Dusty on the other end.

"For heaven's sake! Did I ask you to mow?"

"What else are you callin' about? Not them gnomes again."

Myrtle said, "Yes indeed, the gnomes. I need all of them out in my yard, pronto."

Dusty groaned as if a headache had suddenly been induced.

Miles said, "Are you sure, Myrtle? Remember, it's book club today."

"I'm absolutely positive. It will be a testament to the entire club that Red has been treading on thin ice again."

Dusty said, "What time?"

"Just as soon as you can get over here. And Puddin is supposed to be here this morning, too and I haven't seen hide nor hair of her."

Dusty growled, "It is pretty early."

"Time is relative." Then Myrtle added sternly, "Remind her I'm hosting book club today."

Dusty took that to mean that he should inform Puddin right that second. He hollered the message to her and she hollered back at him.

"She wants ter know if she's invited," said Dusty.

Myrtle said, "Not unless she has time to read *Ethan Frome* and comment intelligently on it in the next few hours."

Dusty relayed this message and Myrtle could hear Puddin's sullen response, herself.

Dusty said, "We'll be there in the next twenty minutes."

"Excellent." Myrtle hung up the phone.

It was more like thirty minutes when Dusty and Puddin showed up. Miles had headed back home to prepare for book club and, Myrtle suspected, take a nap. Puddin's pale features had a surly expression. On the bright side, however, she'd actually brought her own cleaning products. That was often not the case.

Myrtle said, "Now Puddin, as you know, I'm hosting book club shortly. You know what you need to do to make the house presentable."

Puddin grumbled under her breath.

"It won't take you long if you just attack it. Act like the dust is a mortal enemy. Have the vacuum be your weapon."

Puddin's expression indicated that she believed Myrtle had suffered a small stroke. She sauntered into the back of the house with her bucket and supplies.

"Dusty, I'd like you to pull out as many of the gnomes as you can."

Dusty groaned, but nodded. "What did he do this time?"

"Red, you mean? He's being completely impossible. He's acting like Miles had something to do with this murder he's investigating."

Dusty gave a startled cackle and shook his head. "Yeah. Believe me, I know some bad guys. Miles ain't one of them."

"No, he's not. Red really should be focusing his time and attention on the woman who was seeing Jax."

Dusty looked interested. "That Eloise? Ain't that her name?"

Myrtle frowned. "How very perceptive of you, Dusty. Do you know her? And Jax?"

Dusty spat on the ground, which seemed to be a commentary on Eloise, Jax, or both of them. "Yep. Was Jax's yard man. Lots of comin's and goin's over there."

"Women, you mean?" asked Myrtle.

"Yep. Especially that Eloise lately."

Myrtle said, "It's obvious to me that Eloise has a criminal mind. Red hasn't paid nearly enough attention to her as a suspect. It's all very annoying."

Dusty seemed entirely too eager to chat and Myrtle realized the clock was ticking. "Okay, well, chop-chop! There's no time like the present. I've just had a fabulous idea and need to get started on it."

Dusty sighed and loped off for the storage shed that held Myrtle's extensive gnome collection. Inside, Puddin was lackadaisically wiping down the bathroom. Myrtle took out magic markers and paper from her desk and took them to her kitchen table. She proceeded to make signs and then regarded them admiringly when she was done.

Puddin came in, looking pouty. Then she stared curiously at Myrtle's signs. "Whacha doin' there?"

Myrtle showed her. The signs said *Miles is innocent!* and *Free Miles!*

Puddin looked interested. "Miles is in trouble?" There was a gleeful expression on her face. In her experience, men like Miles usually weren't.

"Not really. Red knows better than to really consider Miles as a suspect. But this will serve as a reminder to him and everyone in town that Miles isn't the problem."

Myrtle took the signs and some tape and walked out her front door. She arranged it so that several of the gnomes were holding signs. Then she looked at her handiwork, pleased.

Dusty grunted as he continued lugging gnomes into the few bare places in the yard. "Reckon that'll send Red a message."

"Unless he's very dim, which Red isn't." Myrtle paused. "What did you think of Jax?"

Dusty shrugged. "Thought a lot of himself. Said whatever was on his mind."

"Yes, that's the impression I had of him, too. But I didn't know him as well as you probably did."

Dusty spat on the ground again. It appeared to be a visceral reaction to Jax's name.

"You clearly didn't like him much," said Myrtle.

"Nope. But he did pay me on time and stayed out of my way. Some people don't. They hang out their windows and point out what they want me to do."

"That would be very annoying. So it sounds like Jax wasn't all bad," said Myrtle, hoping to provoke a denial to that statement.

But Dusty just shrugged again. "Guess not." He seemed to think about spitting again, but then just bit his lip instead.

Myrtle walked back inside to supervise Puddin. This was a good thing because Puddin appeared to be opening a bag of chips.

"Those are mine, Puddin!" called out Myrtle.

Puddin jumped and dropped the bag of chips on the floor in the process. She glared at Myrtle. "Shouldn't be sneaking up behind people."

"Nonsense. It's my house. You only reacted that way because you were about to eat my potato chips."

Puddin said defensively, "I ain't had breakfast yet!"

"Well, potato chips are hardly the breakfast of champions. Here, I have a couple of granola bars that should tide you over."

Myrtle went to her pantry, fished in a box, and pulled out two of the bars. Puddin looked suspiciously at them before opening one of them.

"What's all this stuff in them?" she asked.

"Puddin, you're not five years old. It's stuff that's good for you."

This did not alleviate Puddin's concerns.

Myrtle sighed and pulled the box back out. "Chia seeds, granola, almond butter, and chewy dried cranberries," she read aloud.

Puddin scowled at the bars.

"I think you'll find them very filling. You probably won't be hungry for the rest of the day."

"Prob'ly not. Because I'll be feelin' sick," drawled Puddin. But she dutifully ate the bars, chewing tentatively as she worked.

Myrtle spent the time working on her short book club talk about Edith Wharton and *Ethan Frome*. Miles had warned her to keep her talk "accessible." This had given her pause. She'd planned on speaking to the group exactly as she had her high school students back in the day. Now she was wondering if her book club might not be up to par with studious teenagers. She might have to dial back some of her points about the symbolism present in the winter setting and the imagery Wharton chose to portray it.

She was mulling this over when Dusty came back inside. "Your feet, Dusty!" hollered Puddin from the kitchen.

Dusty glared at his wife. "My feet is fine," he protested.

"Look at what yer trackin' in," said Puddin with fiery eyes. She grabbed him by the arm and shoved him out of the house.

"Well, that was one effective way of preventing a re-vacuuming job," muttered Myrtle.

Puddin picked up the few bits of grass from the floor and flung them out of the front door behind Dusty. "Ain't gonna do no more vacuumin' today."

"And you're not hungry, are you?" asked Myrtle.

"Nope. I feel like I have cement in my stomach," said Puddin, pushing a lock of dirty-blonde hair from her pale face. "And I reckon I'm done, Miz Myrtle."

"Done?" Myrtle looked around the room. Nothing glistened, but nothing looked neglected, either. She sighed. "I guess it'll have to do. They'll be coming over soon, anyway."

"Ain't you got to put food out?" This was the main reason Puddin wanted to come to book club, Myrtle surmised. That and the fact that she tended to get lots of attention when she did attend.

Myrtle shook her head. "They changed the rules. Now the hostess doesn't have to provide food . . . only the attending members."

Puddin tilted her head to the side and considered Myrtle thoughtfully through narrowed eyes. "When did they start up this new rule?"

"Last month," said Myrtle with a shrug.

Puddin snickered. "Okay. Well, I better be goin'."

Myrtle followed her outside to see Dusty sitting in the truck already. He gestured to the gnomes, which were all lined up in every possible spot in her yard. Myrtle nodded to him and gave him a thumbs-up.

Chapter Six

A mere fifteen minutes later, the book club members started showing up. Tippy came in first, which she liked to do since she was club president. She was dressed elegantly in black and white and had her hair pulled up in a chignon. Tippy had recently become elected to local office and Myrtle was relieved to see that the town council had started behaving itself with Tippy in the meetings. She tended to have a calming effect on groups.

Tippy had a couple of tote bags and a smile for Myrtle.

"I brought along the punch bowl and all the paper and plastic utensils. I think it would be best if we didn't leave you anything to clean up, under the circumstances."

Myrtle figured "the circumstances" involved Myrtle's considerable age and the ineptitude of her housecleaner. She nodded. "I think that sounds perfect."

Tippy busied herself by setting up the punch and punch-bowl as Blanche arrived behind her. Blanche was also dressed in fancy clothes, but hers looked a bit flashier. She grinned at Tippy and Myrtle. "I think we need to spike the punch, ladies, don't you?"

Tippy gave her a patient but restraining look. "I have the feeling that wouldn't be a good idea. That's happened before, as you might remember, and the outcome was fairly impactful."

The impact involved most of the ladies having to call for rides home from book club and Miles falling asleep in his chair.

Myrtle said, "I don't have anything appropriate for spiking punch, anyway. There's only sherry in my pantry."

Blanche made a face at the idea of spiking the fruit punch (which appeared to include ginger ale, frozen lemonade, and frozen orange juice) with sherry. "No thanks. I guess we'll try to keep on the straight and narrow this time. Although it's tough for some of us."

Myrtle winced as Erma Sherman barreled in. "Hi everyone!" she trilled out.

Blanche hastily muttered something about needing to get something out of her car and hurried out the door. Myrtle gave Erma a small wave before retreating to the kitchen. That left the ever-gracious Tippy to make conversation with Erma as she got the punch together. Myrtle glared suspiciously at the food that Erma brought with her. Somehow, no matter what kind of hors d'oeuvres Erma brought to an event, it always seemed to be accompanied by stale bread or crackers.

Minutes later, Myrtle's living room was full and buzzing with voices. Miles came in and sidled up to Myrtle. "This is quite a big turnout," he murmured to her.

"Indeed it is," said Myrtle. "I expect it's because everyone is eager to discuss *Ethan Frome*. As they should be."

Miles gave her a dubious look.

"I'm going to go ahead and call the meeting to order," she said.

Miles glanced at his watch. "Isn't it a little early to start? Everyone's still eating snacks and getting punch."

Myrtle waved her hand. "They'll be fine. There's likely to be a lot of good conversations about the book so I want to make sure we have as much time as possible."

Looking wary, Miles took his seat.

Myrtle clapped her hands and used her schoolteacher voice to call the room to order. That authoritative note still managed to deliver results and everyone quickly found a seat.

"I'm pleased to see so many of you here today," said Myrtle. She held up her copy of the book, which was tattered from time and lots of use in the classroom. "*Ethan Frome* is such an excellent novel and I'm looking forward to hearing what you all thought of it."

Erma looked stricken. "What? Are you mispronouncing the title, Myrtle?"

"I can assure you that I'm not," said Myrtle coolly.

Erma glanced guiltily over at Sherry, a member who lived down the street. "It's just that I thought you said we were reading *Ellen's Frame*."

Myrtle gritted her teeth. "What on earth would give you that impression?"

Erma sighed. "Well, I've had this ear infection lately. It wasn't so bad at first, but then I realized this clear liquid was—"

Myrtle closed her eyes and waved her hands in the air. "Erma, please."

"Anyway, I guess all that fluid made me a little hard of hearing, that's all. And *Ellen's Frame* was really an excellent book. Didn't you think so, Sherry?"

Myrtle felt her blood pressure rising. This was alarming, since her blood pressure was always excellent, as opposed to Red's. "Sherry? Did you read the wrong book too, Sherry?"

Sherry gave Myrtle an apologetic look. "Sorry. I didn't make the last meeting so I asked Erma when I saw her outside one day."

Myrtle put her hands on her hips. "Who on earth would write a book called *Ellen's Frame*?"

Erma promptly responded, "A man called Eric Sinclair did."

"It's a ridiculous title," said Myrtle.

Miles had his hands over his mouth as if he were trying to keep a laugh from escaping.

Erma said, "Not really. It makes sense once you've read the book. You see, there's a middle-aged woman named Ellen and she has an old picture of her mother in a frame. The more she looks at the picture, the more she realizes there's something very odd about the picture."

"The only thing odd is that it wasn't titled *Ellen's Photo*. That would have made more sense," growled Myrtle. "And I don't want to hear a recap of the story."

"Because you want to read it," said Erma smugly.

"I can assure you that I don't want to read a word of it. The reason I don't want to hear a recap is because that's not the book club selection, Erma."

Sherry, never one to waste a read, said, "I'm with Erma—it was a good book. Maybe it should be our pick for next month."

Blanche said, "I second the motion. It's my month to pick and I haven't done my homework yet to find one."

Myrtle said severely, "It sounds as if *no one* has done their homework. Did the rest of you read *Ethan Frome*?"

Blanche spoke up again, shrugging an elegant shoulder, "I'm going to be completely honest here. I did *not* read the book."

"I can't believe this. We're talking about Edith Wharton, for heaven's sake. It's not like we're parsing Shakespeare. Her style is practically contemporary."

Tippy cleared her throat and said in a cautious voice, "Myrtle, several of the members contacted me to let me know the story was something of a downer."

Myrtle opened her mouth to speak but nothing came out.

Tippy, emboldened by the uncharacteristic lack of sharp response, added, "They said it was full of despair."

Myrtle found her voice again. "It has a love triangle. Everyone in this group is always wanting to read love triangles. What's the difference between reading about love triangles in *Jennifer's Promise* instead of *Ethan Frome*? Who in here actually read the book?"

The women looked at each other nervously. Tippy raised her hand, but not very high. "I did do quite a bit of skimming," she admitted.

Miles raised his hand.

Myrtle said, "Well, I can't hold a discussion on a book with Miles for the next thirty minutes."

Tippy said, "Maybe you should choose a *happier* book next time, Myrtle. Our group has a tough time with doom and gloom. I know you like classic novels, but aren't there any *pleasant* classic novels?"

Myrtle and Miles looked at each other. Pleasantries were often not part of classic novels. Classic novels of any worth, anyway.

Erma said reprovingly, "A *feel-good* story, Myrtle. Aren't there any of those?"

Miles offered, "There's *A Midsummer Night's Dream.*"

The women chorused back, "No Shakespeare!"

Myrtle glared at them. "I'm going to make a pick and I shouldn't have to wait months until it's my turn again. Agreed? Blanche, you can put off *Ellen's Frame* for another month and let me take your turn."

Blanche shrugged again.

"What's your pick?" asked Tippy with some trepidation.

"Oscar Wilde's *The Importance of Being Earnest.*"

Miles looked impressed. "An excellent choice."

"And I expect everyone to read it. There will be a pop quiz." Myrtle leveled her gaze at the room. Everyone shifted uncomfortably in their chairs. "And don't call Tippy at the last minute to tell her that you have headaches and can't come."

Tippy stood up and walked up next to Myrtle. "Everyone, let's give Myrtle a round of applause for preparing a talk today and hosting us. We know you put time into it and we appreciate you."

There was a round of applause while Myrtle, still aggravated, glowered at them all.

The women quickly moved out of their chairs and to the food table, getting small tidbits and talking to each other.

Myrtle sat next to Miles. "Well, that didn't go as expected."

"Didn't it?" asked Miles. "It seems to me it was about par for the course. You really couldn't have thought that they were going to have an enthusiastic and thoughtful discussion on *Ethan Frome*."

"I'm an optimist," said Myrtle.

Myrtle and Miles didn't notice Erma sidling up to them until it was too late.

"Heloooo," sang Erma with her leering smile. "How are the two of you? Having a tete-a-tete?"

Myrtle gave Erma a chilly look. "Just a conversation about how disastrous book club went today. And you didn't help."

Erma gave her donkey-like hee-hawing laugh. "I didn't mishear the book title on purpose. Anyway, it was a weird name for a book. It's not like it's something easy to remember."

"It's the name of the protagonist," said Myrtle, glaring at Erma.

"Well, she has a weird name."

"The protagonist is a man." Myrtle was speaking through gritted teeth.

"Anyway, all's well that ends well," said Erma breezily. "We found a great book to read next time. *Ellen's Frame* will be good for discussion."

Miles said, "Remember, that's going to be the discussion *two* months from now. Myrtle has another pick for next time."

Erma winced. "That's right. Ugh. Hope it's a good book."

"It's a play, actually."

Erma's eyes grew wide. "No! A play like Shakespeare?"

"A play that's not at all like Shakespeare."

Blanche was passing by on her way to the food and turned her head sharply. "What? Myrtle, did you pick Shakespeare for next month? I thought we made the no-Shakespeare rule plain."

"I certainly did not choose Shakespeare," said Myrtle coldly. "This club would be incompatible with the great works of the Bard. I picked a play, and apparently the only plays Erma is familiar with are Shakespeare's."

"Well, that's a relief," said Blanche. "I was starting to think I was going to have to find myself another book club."

Erma said, "Glad that's cleared up. You wouldn't have had anybody come next month, otherwise." She glanced around and then said in a loud whisper, "I wanted to talk to you about what happened. The murder. Were you really on the scene when it happened, Miles?"

Miles gave Erma a horrified look. "No! I wasn't anywhere near Jax's house."

Erma gave her hee-hawing laugh again. "Come on, we know that's not true. You were *seen* there. I have my spies, you know." She gave him a big wink.

Myrtle jumped in. "Your spies clearly have vision issues. Miles wasn't at Jax's house until after Eloise called him to tell him what happened."

"Ohhh. So *Eloise* was at the scene. Sorry about your break-up, by the way, Miles."

Miles was looking longingly at Myrtle's door as if hoping he could somehow teleport out of it and back to the safety of his home.

Myrtle said, "Eloise discovered the body. You're making it sound like she was responsible for Jax's death."

Erma shrugged. "I hear things." She leaned closer and Myrtle and Miles leaned backward in response. "One thing I heard was that Allen West was at Jax's house that evening."

"Allen?" asked Miles, looking a bit shocked. Allen was a friend of Miles's who generally had a quiet life. Getting involved in a murder was not his usual modus operandi.

Myrtle said in a thoughtful voice, "That's interesting. What's his connection to Jax?"

Erma grinned. "They both worked at the community theater. They definitely know each other."

Myrtle was trying to think of a good way to escape when Erma suddenly spotted cake on someone's plate. Erma perked up and hurried away. "Better get some before it's gone," she muttered behind her.

Miles hurriedly stood. "I'm going to go ahead and go before anyone else comes up."

"I'll see you later," said Myrtle as he strode off.

Myrtle stood up too and walked over to make herself a plate of refreshments. Sherry was also there, pouring herself a cup of punch.

"Is it true?" asked Sherry in a hushed voice.

Myrtle frowned. "Is what true?"

"That Eloise broke Miles's heart? I saw the signs you'd put outside. Are they an appeal to Eloise?"

Myrtle thought that "save Miles" and "free Miles" would be very melodramatic signs indeed if they were in regard to a relationship.

Blanche, who had an excellent radar when it came to gossip, quickly appeared beside them. "Is Miles okay?"

Myrtle was opening her mouth to say that Miles was perfectly fine, not that it was any of their business, when she shut it back again. Perhaps making Miles look particularly pitiful might be beneficial. There could even be sympathy casseroles involved to express their sorrow over Miles's broken heart.

She surreptitiously glanced behind her to make sure Miles hadn't suddenly returned and said, "It's been just awful. Poor Miles has been so miserable."

Sherry's and Blanche's eyes grew wide. "I *thought* so," said Sherry.

Blanche nodded. "Miles is always so sensitive. I've never met a man who enjoyed poetry the way he does. Of *course* he fell apart when Eloise dumped him."

"Did he? Did he fall apart?" asked Sherry rather breathlessly.

"Like a cheap suit," said Myrtle, looking sad.

Sherry and Blanche looked at each other and shook their heads. Blanche excused herself and hurried off toward a group of women clustered around Tippy. The news would spread fast.

Sherry said slowly, "Do you think Miles would like some baked goods, Myrtle?"

"Oh, I'm certain he would. You know how bachelors are. I don't think Miles has ever baked anything a day in his life."

Sherry mused, "Maybe a pound cake. Or I could make one of my blueberry pound cake loaves—he could have those for breakfast."

Myrtle smiled. Sherry's breakfast loaves were locally famous. "I'm sure he'd enjoy one, Sherry. That's so sweet of you."

Book club didn't last much longer. The women of book club exited quickly to take to their kitchens.

The next morning, Myrtle's phone rang at nine o'clock.

Miles said, "Myrtle, do you know anything about why food might be arriving at my door?"

"Food?" asked Myrtle vaguely, as if the word were foreign to her.

"Yes. Baked goods, in particular."

"Hm. Well, you know people love baking. Maybe it's stress relief for them. After all, there's been a murder of a fairly popular resident. They could be trying to rid themselves of tension by being creative. Because baking is creative."

Myrtle heard the sound of a doorbell on Miles's end of the line. He said in a grouchy tone, "I have the feeling you're somehow behind this."

"You should answer your door, Miles. It's not good to let food sit outside on the doorstep."

Miles muttered a goodbye and hung up. Myrtle smiled to herself.

Chapter Seven

Myrtle was just finishing up her crossword when her own doorbell rang.

"Hi there," she said cheerily to Miles. He was holding a tote bag and had a rather grim expression.

He carefully carried the tote bag to the kitchen as Myrtle followed behind him, a smile tugging at her lips. Miles unpacked Sherry's blueberry pound cake loaf, a plate of cookies, lemon bars, crustless pimento cheese sandwiches, and a casserole.

"Gracious, what a lot of goodies," said Myrtle, rubbing her hands together. "Are you sharing?"

"Of course I am. There's no way a person living on their own could be expected to eat this much food before it went bad. But I'd like to hear an explanation for this unprecedented generosity by our fellow book club members."

Myrtle took down a couple of plates from her cabinets. "They didn't tell you why they were bringing food?"

"Apparently, they were trying to be sensitive," said Miles unhappily. "They were tiptoeing around the subject. I figured that you either told them I'd lost a close relative, or that you had somehow exaggerated my breakup with Eloise."

Myrtle used a knife to cut up the pound cake loaf. "Oh, they wanted to believe you had a broken heart. I was about to tell them that *you* were the one who broke up with *her*. But it made you sound rather unchivalrous."

"You were the one who encouraged me to do it!"

"Yes, but it was a tale that was going to suffer in the retelling. It sounded so much better to just give them what they wanted to hear. . . that poor Miles had been dumped by the ruthless Eloise and had his heart broken in two."

Miles closed his eyes. "Oh no."

"You know how they don't get the point of things. Themes, symbolism, anything that requires intuition completely bypasses these women during book club. So they thought the signs on the gnomes meant something specific to Eloise."

Miles, who still had his eyes closed, gave a groan like someone who was in deep pain. Perhaps appendicitis-level pain.

Then he opened his eyes. "About those gnomes. I think the signs can go, Myrtle. I appreciate the point you were trying to make, though. I'm sure Red has already gotten it by now."

"Well, it's completely ridiculous that he would consider you a murderer. The absurdity! He's completely wasting his time by investigating you when he should be hunting down the actual perpetrator."

Miles shifted uncomfortably. "Do you think he *is* doing that? Investigating me?"

Myrtle shrugged. "How do I know? He never tells me anything."

They spent the next few moments happily eating pound cake and sipping at their coffee.

"What are you doing today?" asked Miles curiously.

Myrtle waggled her fingers at him. "I'm getting my nails done."

"Well, that sounds like a remarkable thing to have on your agenda for the day. I don't recall you caring very much about manicures."

Myrtle snorted. "I don't. But I figured it might be an excellent way to speak with Nicole Jackson."

Miles's face reflected surprise before he beamed at her. "Myrtle, I think that's an excellent idea. Well done."

"You don't have to sound so surprised about it. You know I do like to speak to all my suspects and Nicole definitely qualifies as a suspect. She wanted her father to sell his property on the lake. She apparently needs money. It stands to reason that she's a good suspect."

"Oh, I know," said Miles hurriedly. "It's just that ordinarily, you want to bring the family members food."

Myrtle gave him an annoyed look. "Surely I'm allowed to switch things up."

"Of course you are." Miles gave a happy smile, which seemed to annoy Myrtle further.

"You act as though people aren't delighted to receive my casseroles."

Miles hastily interjected, "Naturally they are. But I suppose sometimes people get quite a *bit* of food. That could be stressful, too. I'm currently completely snowed under with baked goods, for instance. And I have the terrible feeling I'm expected to write thank-you notes."

"Thank you notes are a must," said Myrtle sternly.

"I'll get right on them. Likely while you're getting your nails painted." He glanced over at Myrtle's hands and their sturdy, no-nonsense short nails. "Are you absolutely sure that Nicole Jackson will be there today? After all, she just lost her father."

"I called and made an appointment specifically with her, so she's definitely working. I guess she needs the money. Or maybe she's there as a distraction." She looked at the clock. "Now I should be heading along."

"Where is the nail salon?"

"Downtown. Not too far. I don't need a ride."

They both stood up and Miles said regretfully, "I suppose I should go ahead and tackle those thank-you notes then."

"There's no time like the present."

Miles wandered slowly back to his house as Myrtle got her purse and her cane and set off down the street toward downtown.

The nail salon was situated in a cheerfully-painted brick building with flowers in the front window. And it was absolutely inundated with people. Myrtle blinked at them as she walked in. As far as she was aware, she'd never had her nails done, ever. But here were people from all walks of life getting manicures and pedicures. It was like a whole other world.

The receptionist checked her in and Nicole came up to join her. She had dark hair and eyes and seemed to be in her late-thirties. She wore a black and white outfit that Myrtle suspected was quite expensive. And her nails were quite dramatic in both color and length.

"Miss Myrtle," said Nicole with a smile. "I haven't seen you in a long time. My dad always had good things to say about you."

Myrtle was surprised to hear this. She didn't remember Jax being particularly interested in her one way or another. "Well, that was sweet of him. I was so sorry to hear of his passing, dear. I know this must be such a hard time for you."

Nicole gave her a tight smile. "It has been. But everyone has been kind." She paused for a second and then added. "Should we get started with your nails?"

Myrtle glanced around the room. "Sure. What do I need to do?"

Nicole's eyes, framed by lush false eyelashes grew wide. "You've never had a manicure?"

"No, I do my own nails. But when you're my age, you need to pay your bucket list particular attention."

"A manicure is on your bucket list?" Nicole seemed a bit doubtful at that, but, to Myrtle's relief, not at all suspicious.

"Why not? It's something I haven't done before."

Nicole said, "Okay. Well, the first thing you need to do is to head over to this wall over here and pick your color."

Myrtle walked over and stood before a huge number of nail polish bottles. "Heavens. Where should I start?"

Nicole said, "I'm guessing you might want something fairly conservative. Maybe a light pink? The advantage there is that it can chip and no one can really even tell."

"That sounds sensible," said Myrtle.

Nicole quirked an eyebrow. "Of course, sometimes we don't want to be conservative or sensible. We just want to do something a little different. Since this is a bucket list item, maybe you'd like to do something a bit more radical."

Myrtle was intrigued. "What do you have in mind?"

Nicole gave her a considering look. "Do you like robin's egg blue?"

"Generally? Yes. I wouldn't have thought about having it on my fingernails, though."

Nicole said, "Oh, I think it would make a fun statement."

"It would certainly make a *statement*."

"We have a bottle with sparkles in it. So your fingertips will look magical," said Nicole.

Myrtle's mind was already heading to upcoming events and whether robin's egg blue fingernail polish would be entirely appropriate. "The only thing, dear, is your poor father's funeral. I'm not sure I should wear something like that for that particular occasion."

Nicole laughed. "Are you kidding? Dad would have *loved* it. He'd be the first one to say that a funeral required that everyone needed cheering up. Besides, this isn't a normal funeral."

"Then I believe that color with the sparkles would do very well, Nicole, thanks."

Nicole found the bottle and she and Myrtle headed to a table that was set up already and Nicole started briskly shaping and filing Myrtle's nails. Nicole said, "Yes, this will be the perfect tribute for Dad."

Myrtle said, "You mentioned that Jax isn't having a normal funeral. Now I'm curious."

Nicole's wry expression indicated that she suspected Myrtle was *always* curious. "It's going to be really different. And I guess it's not really a funeral at all—it's more of a celebration of life ceremony. Dad is being cremated. But he left really detailed instructions on everything he wanted done, so I'm following it to a T. The last thing I need is for Dad to haunt me for not doing exactly what he wanted."

"Is it going to be at the church?" asked Myrtle.

"Oh, no. You know how Dad was. He wants the service in his yard. So I've got a place that usually does weddings coming to set up tables and chairs. Let's hope we have good weather or else it's going to be a disaster."

"When is it again?"

"It's tomorrow," said Nicole.

"Tomorrow!" It all seemed rather abrupt. Myrtle wasn't even sure how Nicole had been able to plan and execute an unusual funeral in such short time.

Nicole shrugged. "It's my day off, so it seemed to work out well. Because it's the middle of the week, there were discounts for the catering. And since it's a celebration of life ceremony, it doesn't matter that the police aren't quite finished with Dad's body yet."

The mention of the body was rather sobering and they were both quiet for a few moments.

Myrtle finally said slowly, "I can't help but wonder what happened to Jax, Nicole. He was always such a vibrant man—it's hard to believe he's gone."

Myrtle saw that flash in Nicole's eyes again and knew exactly what she was thinking. She was now *positive* that Myrtle was a nosy old lady. Nicole said casually, "I know. That's how I've been feeling, too. I keep thinking that I can just pick up the phone and give him a call. It's unbelievable that he's not around anymore. I was so shocked when the cops told me about it. I'd worked late here, picked up takeout, then went home to watch TV. I kept thinking that if I'd just gone over to check on Dad, none of this would have happened."

Myrtle said briskly, "You couldn't have known. Jax wasn't the sort of person who really required being checked on, anyway."

Nicole snorted. "You've got that right. He was fiercely independent and let me know when I was getting into his business too much. He and I had that in common, at least. I was actually a lot more like my mom than Dad, but I did get his independent spirit."

"How long ago has it been since your mom passed?"

"Gosh, it's been twelve or more years." Nicole was quiet for a minute as she worked on Myrtle's right hand. Then she said, "I can't believe time has flown that quickly. It's just another reminder that I need to leave Bradley."

This was a sentiment that Myrtle had heard over the years from many a young resident of the town. Some of them did make it out and some of them couldn't seem to get motivated enough to actually leave. "Where would you go?"

"Atlanta."

"Really?" Myrtle couldn't imagine living in Atlanta. The times she'd been through there it seemed as if everyone on the highway had wanted to be in her lane, even if she were already occupying it. "Would you have a salon there?"

Nicole shook her head. "I'm really interested in fashion, mostly."

This was an area outside of Myrtle's purview. "Would that mean working in retail?"

"Well, I'd like to be a fashion buyer. That's someone who picks out clothes from designers to stock in boutiques and department stores."

Myrtle said, "I'd imagine there'd be a good deal more demand for that in Atlanta than Bradley."

"Exactly. So I've been wanting to leave and move to Atlanta. But I've had a hard time saving enough money to make the trip over there. I don't know anyone in Atlanta, so I wouldn't have a roommate to cut costs. And it's tough socking away cash when I don't make very much working here."

Myrtle reflected that she might need to give Nicole a bit more of a tip than she'd planned on.

"That's why I was hoping my dad could lend me the money."

Myrtle said, "Was he able to do that?"

Nicole made a face. "He *wanted* to. But he just didn't have that kind of cash on hand. He'd never been great at financial stuff and didn't care whether he had money or not. He just liked having fun. Not even *expensive* fun . . . just hanging out and listening to music and drinking beer. That's why I was so aggravated with him about the property."

Myrtle carefully arranged her expression so it wouldn't reveal the fact that she already knew about the real estate developer wanting to buy Jax's land. "Property?"

Nicole sighed as she put Myrtle's other hand into a bowl to soak. "Just the property he lives on. The house isn't anything fancy, but he owned several acres smack-dab on the lake. A developer offered him a big chunk of money if he'd sell it to them for condos or apartments or something."

"I'm guessing Jax said no to that."

Nicole's face flushed with remembered anger. "Unfortunately. He could be a very stubborn guy when he wanted to be."

"Did you try to talk him into taking the developer up on it?"

Nicole sighed. "Yeah, I sure did. It led to some nasty arguments between the two of us, which I feel really awful about now. But my dad didn't understand me at all—we were completely different in a lot of ways. I tried to explain my goals to him, but he just didn't get them. He wasn't into fashion, of course. But besides that, he also didn't have any higher aspirations. He'd never wanted to leave Bradley."

Myrtle nodded, hoping the slight encouragement would keep Nicole talking. And, indeed, Nicole didn't seem to be one of those manicurists who was happy with silence.

"Anyway, that was Dad—just living in the moment. At least I know that he died happy because Dad was *always* happy. Always content. He made me feel like there was something wrong with me for wanting something different."

Myrtle said, "Well, there isn't, dear. Different strokes for different folks. But tell me . . . have things changed now? Is the deal with the developer still on the table?"

Nicole gave her a wry look. "This is going to sound awful, but that was the first call I made after Dad died. The developer said the deal was absolutely still on the table, so I plan on selling the lot. It's going to take a while, of course, to work its way through probate, but I'm not in any real hurry. Now that I know

I can do what I want, I'm happy to wait a little while. That's the only good thing that's come out of all this."

Myrtle said, "Well, I know you miss him. Whenever I saw him out and about, he was always a bright spot in my day." This was a bit of a stretch. Myrtle had found him rather self-centered and hedonistic.

Nicole gave her a smile. "Thanks, Miss Myrtle. Everybody has been really nice. Now if the police can just figure out who did it." She flushed a little and said, "Sorry. I didn't mean anything by that. I know Red is your son."

"I tend to agree with you that the police are very poky in figuring these things out sometimes. You don't have any ideas about who could have been behind this, do you?"

Nicole carefully painted the blue polish on Myrtle's fingertips. "Nope. Although I do know Dad wasn't getting along real well with Eloise."

"Really?" Myrtle might have sounded a touch eager. There was a part of her that would like to see Eloise thrown under the proverbial bus.

"I know, right? They always seemed like they were getting along great when they were out in public together. And who knows—maybe they had one of those relationships where it was sort of fiery. Or maybe they put an act on when people could see them together. Anyway, I'd run by Dad's house a few days before he died to try to convince him again to sell his property. I'd found a really cute place for sale in town that looked like the kind of house he'd really like."

"And Eloise was with your dad?"

Nicole snorted. "Well, she was screaming at him, actually. I didn't even make it into the house. I parked the car and got out and there was Eloise yelling at him and Dad just sort of looked bemused with his arms folded. Then I saw that Marigold was just inside the house."

Myrtle nodded. "I understand that Marigold was having an affair with Jax."

Nicole rolled her eyes. "Yeah. That was Dad's business and I didn't offer my opinion on it. But I wasn't surprised that Eloise was furious about it. It would have been one thing if he'd been upfront with her. But apparently, Eloise thought she was in an exclusive relationship with my father."

Myrtle raised her eyebrows. "Did she? Well, that's rather extraordinary. My friend Miles thought he was in an exclusive relationship with Eloise. But Eloise acted as if it wasn't any big deal that she was seeing someone else."

"She's probably one of those people where it only matters that *she* isn't being cheated on. She doesn't care that she's cheating on other people."

Myrtle said dryly, "That sounds about right. She's not exactly a real catch, is she?"

"It's not the kind of relationship I'd want to be in, that's for sure. But it worked for Dad, obviously. And, like I said, I didn't say anything to him about it. He was a widower, after all. But I have to admit I wasn't too keen on him getting married again." Nicole carefully wiped away a stray bit of paint from Myrtle's cuticle.

Myrtle said, "I can imagine."

"It seems silly to say it, but it would have felt disrespectful to my mother's memory."

Myrtle couldn't help but wonder if Nicole was being disingenuous. Maybe Nicole was more concerned about losing her dad's property than anything else.

"Besides Eloise, I did know about one other issue Dad was having with somebody. Allen."

"Allen?" asked Myrtle.

"Allen-from-the-theater," said Nicole with a shrug. "I don't really know anything else about him except that my father was complaining about him."

"You know, I do remember that your dad was a local thespian."

Nicole furrowed her brows and Myrtle explained, "I mean, he's part of the community theater in Bradley. Is Mr. Toucan still in charge of the theater?"

"I have no idea. I've never really been that interested in the theater, myself. I used to do stuff over there when I was a kid for these day camps my parents would put me in. My mom always said I was so dramatic that I needed to go into the theater. But I never really got into it, dramatic or not. I was just glad that it was something Dad enjoyed. It's good to be part of something, isn't it? Anyway, I know he was in some productions over there and did some other stuff with the theater, too—maybe was an usher or something like that. He talked about the people he knew over there and the friends he'd made, but I must not have been listening very carefully because it didn't really make an impression on me."

"What did Jax say about Allen? You said Jax was complaining about him?"

Nicole made a face. "I guess I wasn't listening very hard again. But yeah—Dad wasn't happy with him. They'd had some kind of tiff, but I got the impression that the tiff was all on Allen's side. That's all I really remember." She tilted her head to the side and considered Myrtle's brightly-painted nails through narrowed eyes and then nodded at her handiwork. "All right. We're going to want to put you under the nail dryer for a few minutes to let the paint set. What do you think about them?"

Myrtle wasn't completely sure what to think about her nails. Her hands looked strangely foreign to her. But she had to admit that she felt happy when she looked at them. And sort of . . . peppy.

"They're sassy looking," said Myrtle.

Nicole burst out laughing. "They are, aren't they? And is that okay?"

Myrtle waggled her fingers, peering at them. "I think so. Yes, definitely. After all, you said Jax's memorial service is going to be a lively affair."

"You'll fit in perfectly," said Nicole.

Chapter Eight

Miles's eyes were wide as he saw Myrtle's fingernails. "Wow."

Myrtle smirked at him. "Aren't they colorful?"

Miles was relieved that she gave him an appropriate word to latch onto. "They are, for sure."

"I feel very hip and young all of a sudden. Maybe I should get a manicure more often."

Miles nodded slowly. "Sure—why not?"

"I suppose the only downside is the fact that it costs rather a lot of money. It's surprising, actually, how very much they cost. And then you need to tip, on top of that. I gave Nicole a very generous tip and now I'm going to have to live very leanly the rest of the week until my check comes in."

Miles raised his eyebrows. "You gave her a big tip? Was that because she did such a good job?"

"No. Well, I did think she did a good job. But it was mainly because it sounded like times were tough for Nicole and she has big plans."

"Isn't she set to receive an inheritance from Jax?" Miles pushed his glasses up his nose.

"Yes, but that's going to take forever. As a financial advisor, you should remember that."

"Engineer." Miles's tone was cool.

"Right. Anyway, she's not going to get that money right away—not even close. The property has to go through probate and then she has to sell the property. It's all going to take a very long time." Myrtle spread her fingers out in front of her and admired them.

They were in Miles's house. He had made tomato sandwiches for them both. They liked different types of mayonnaise, but now Miles kept a small bottle of Myrtle's favorite in his fridge for occasions such as this.

"Do you think that Nicole could possibly have murdered Jax?" Miles's brow furrowed at the thought.

"Of course she could have. She's a very strong-minded young woman and she wants to have enough money to leave Bradley and move to her dream city."

"Which is?" Miles quirked an eyebrow again.

"Atlanta."

Miles said, "Hm. I wouldn't have thought Atlanta would qualify as anyone's dream city, but I haven't been there for a little while. What's she wanting to do there?"

"Something to do with fashion. I don't know much about fashion, but I'd have thought New York would have been a better spot, wouldn't you?"

Miles nodded. "Except for the cost of New York. If she needed money for a move to Atlanta, a move to New York would *really* require some saving up."

"She also admitted being at odds with her dad over his property. Nicole said that they were just completely different people who couldn't understand each other's goals."

"Jax had goals?" asked Miles doubtfully.

"Jax's goals were to enjoy himself in the same house where he'd lived for decades," said Myrtle. "Goals don't have to be lofty things, you know."

"Although it sounds as if Nicole's are."

They considered this for a few moments. "I suppose she could have gotten very frustrated with Jax and lashed out at him," said Myrtle. "After all, in her mind, he was holding her back from doing something she thinks she'll find great fulfillment in."

"It's hard to imagine," said Miles.

Myrtle said, "Well, who do you think could have done it?"

Miles was quiet for a few moments. "I can't picture any of the suspects killing Jax."

Myrtle gave him a stern look. "That's because you still have a soft spot for Eloise."

"I promise you, I don't. However, I can't quite picture her as a rabid killer, either."

Myrtle said, "She might not have been *rabid*. She might simply have been pushed a little too far. Jax was like that. He pushed people's buttons by just being himself. Everything he did was geared to his own enjoyment. He might possibly have been the most self-centered person I've ever met."

Miles thought about this for a few moments. "I can see that. I mean, he was a lot of fun to be with, of course. He was always laughing."

"Naturally. Because he was pleasing himself. But sometimes, in the course of pleasing oneself, one ends up hurting others."

"And you're intimating that Eloise was one of his victims," said Miles.

"Absolutely. And Nicole confirmed it." When Myrtle mentioned Nicole, her gaze pulled back with satisfaction to her robin's egg blue nails and she wiggled her fingers again.

"Did she? What did she say?" Miles suddenly looked a bit more alert. Perhaps, having dated a possible murderer made him worried he could be accused of having bad judgment.

"Nicole said that she'd visited her father a few days before his death and Eloise was screaming at him. The reason she was doing so was apparently because Marigold was inside with Jax and it was obvious they were in a relationship."

Miles tilted his head to one side. "I thought everyone in town allegedly knew that Marigold and Jax were having an affair."

Myrtle shrugged. "*There are none so blind as those who will not see.*"

Miles blinked at her. It was rather unusual for Myrtle to quote scripture to him.

"Anyway, that would explain why Eloise was so angry. She didn't know that Marigold and Jax were still seeing each other. Eloise seemed to think she and Jax were in an exclusive relationship, according to Nicole."

Miles's brow furrowed. "Well, she *wasn't* in an exclusive relationship. She was also seeing me. How could she be angry with Jax for doing the same thing she was? Seeing someone on the side?"

"I guess Eloise thinks she can feel any old way she wants to," said Myrtle with a sniff. "It's rather childish of her. But then, I'd expect that of Eloise."

Miles said dryly, "Yes, I gathered you don't like her."

"The point is that Eloise could certainly have killed Jax if she was that angry. Maybe she went home and brooded on it for a while then returned to hash it out with Jax. He could have said something that really made her angry and she attacked him."

Miles still seemed rather unsettled by the mental image of all this. Myrtle said with a shrug, "Or, if you prefer, Allen could have done it."

"Allen West?"

"The very one."

"Did Nicole say he was on the outs with Jax?" asked Miles.

"She did, although she had no idea what it was about. She didn't even know Allen's last name, but I knew who it was when she mentioned the theater. I know Allen's been very involved in the theater for decades."

"It's his favorite thing," said Miles solemnly. "Although he does also enjoy scrabble."

Myrtle nodded. She was aware that Miles was very successful in scrabble-playing groups in Bradley. It was unspoken between them that Myrtle was rather too good at the game. They didn't play together anymore. In fact, no one in town would, so Myrtle had taken to playing against the computer. If the computer could have quit playing with her, it would have, too.

"He's still a friend of yours, then?"

Miles said, "I'd call him a good acquaintance."

"Could we go pay him a visit?"

Miles said, "I don't think acquaintances drop in on one another. Especially if one is wanting to interrogate the other about murder." He looked at his watch. "But I can tell you where Allen is right this very moment."

"How perceptive of you, Miles!"

"It's only because he's always in the same spot this time every day. He'll be sitting on the benches near the diner with another couple of the old guys. We could invite him to lunch with us."

Myrtle smiled at him and stood up. "What an excellent idea. And I've had a hankering for a pimento cheese dog with chili fries lately."

Miles looked a little green. "I don't know how you handle that much grease. And processed meats."

"I'm positive the diner doesn't use hot dogs with nitrates and nitrites," said Myrtle breezily.

Miles's expression indicated that he wasn't so sure.

Minutes later, they saw that Allen was indeed sitting on a bench in downtown Bradley with a couple of old fellows. Allen waved when he saw Miles walking up and nodded politely to Myrtle. He had thinning white hair and was dressed very neatly—almost as neatly as Miles. But his eyes had lost their usual twinkle and spark and the lines in his face had settled into frowns of dissatisfaction. Something was definitely wrong and Myrtle doubted it was the fact that Jax was gone.

"Hi there, Miles, how are you doing?" he asked, sounding a bit perkier than he looked.

"Just fine, thanks. Myrtle and I were about to have lunch—would you like to join us?"

He seemed to hesitate and Myrtle wondered if he was on a budget. Since she was on a budget, especially after her manicure, she said, "Do join us, Allen. It's Miles's treat."

Miles gave them both a tight smile.

Allen hopped up with alacrity and said, "Thanks! That sounds awesome. See you later, guys." And he quickly left the other old boys on the bench to their own devices.

Usually, they had to wait to be seated, but today there was a booth available right away for them. Allen glanced over the menu hungrily while Miles and Myrtle waited.

"Y'all already know what you want?" he asked.

Miles said, "Myrtle made a pick about twenty minutes ago and I always get the salad."

Allen made a face. "Are the salads even good here? The specialty of the house is fried food."

"The salad is always fresh." It was about as good of a compliment as you could make about a salad.

After they placed their orders, Myrtle gave Miles a prompting look. Miles apparently didn't feel much like being pushy. He said, "So, how have you been, Allen?"

Allen, luckily, seemed to be in the mood to talk about his problems. "Oh, I've not been doing so great. Well, you know how it is. If it's Tuesday, it's the dermatologist. If it's Wednesday, it's the dentist. Lots of medical things going on. But what I'm most upset about is my work at the theater."

"Oh?" asked Miles mildly.

Myrtle asked, "What is it that you do at the theater?"

"I'm afraid it's past tense now," said Allen sadly. "It's all over for me now because I was let go. But I used to do absolutely everything there. I'd work on sets, act, advertise, be an usher, help Toucan with the books, run errands—whatever needed to be done."

"Why on earth would Mr. Toucan dispense with such a valuable member of his staff?" asked Myrtle crisply. "Has he lost his mind?"

"He was lied to," said Allen. "And he couldn't seem to see the truth. But I wasn't a member of his staff. There really *was* no paid staff there. I was just a volunteer."

"More like a super volunteer," muttered Myrtle.

Miles frowned. "I don't understand. What happened?"

Allen sighed and rubbed his face with both hands. "Oh, it's been awful. You know how Jax was also at the theater a lot."

"Were you friends?" asked Myrtle.

"We were friendly. I wouldn't have called us friends since we never did anything together outside of the theater. But we did spend a good deal of time together when we were at the theater."

Myrtle said, "What do you make of his sudden death?"

Allen said, "Well, I'm certainly concerned. It's a horrible thing to happen in a quiet neighborhood like his." But there was a discernible note of smugness in his voice and something else, besides. Maybe schadenfreude.

"You did know where he lived, then?"

Allen blinked in confusion. "Just because I had to go by there sometimes on theater business. He'd paint sets and I'd pick them up in my truck and take them back to the theater. He did a pretty good job with them," said Allen grudgingly.

Miles said, "What did Jax have to do with your being let go at the theater?"

Allen's face darkened. "He lied. He said that he'd caught me pilfering money from the till."

Myrtle's and Miles's eyes opened wide.

"That's right. Then he told Toucan that I'd seen Jax come in and that I'd put the money right back. But the damage was already done by then. Toucan just didn't trust me anymore. I couldn't stand being over there with him watching me all the time like he thought I was going to take something. Before I could quit volunteering, he asked me not to come back."

"Why would Jax do something like that?" asked Myrtle.

They stopped talking while the waitress put down their food.

As soon as she walked away, Allen said viciously, "Because that's the kind of person he was. A mean one. Just look at the way he treated women—with absolutely no respect. The guy wasn't normal, I tell you. I don't like speaking ill of the dead, but I can definitely see where someone could want to take Jax out. He messed with too many people. At some point, someone was going to bite him back. But it wasn't me."

"Did you ever see the women he dated at the theater?" asked Myrtle. Allen nodded and she asked, "What was your perspective on them?"

Allen gave a short laugh. "I thought they were too nice to be seeing Jax. I even told both of them—warned them off. I tried to explain the kind of person Jax was because I'd seen his behavior repeated year after year with different women. I said they were going to end up being hurt."

"Do you think they might have told Jax that you'd warned them off?" asked Miles slowly. "Could that be why Jax lied about your taking money?"

This apparently hadn't occurred to Allen. He made a face. "Maybe." He then proceeded to comfort himself by gulping down large quantities of food. "Anyway, it didn't do any good. Marigold and Eloise kept dating Jax." He looked at Miles. "Sorry, Miles. I know Eloise was your girl for a while."

"Not really," said Miles with a sigh.

"Jax didn't care a thing for them . . . it was evident in the way he was talking about them. He only cared about himself. But those two women weren't all softness and light, either. I wouldn't be surprised if something happened to push one of them over the edge."

Myrtle said, "So you think Marigold or Eloise killed Jax."

"Maybe. Or it could have been Jax's daughter. What's-her-name. Nicole. She has a hard face. Wears too much makeup. She was always after Jax to do something with his property, too—she wouldn't leave him alone about it. I guess all those expensive clothes and purses and things add up and she's short on money. But yeah, I still think it's probably one of the women he was seeing who finally did him in."

Miles asked, "How is Mr. Toucan handling all the different roles you'd filled?"

"Well, he's in a pickle now. But he'd had Jax take over them all."

Myrtle said, "That seems odd to me. Jax was this laid-back, happy-go-lucky kind of guy. He didn't seem like the sort who'd want to do that much work."

Allen shrugged. "It wasn't really work to Jax, like it wasn't really work to me. The theater was a fun place. I kind of felt as if I was playing all day long. I think Jax felt the same way."

Miles said, "Can't you go back now and ask Mr. Toucan to reinstate you? Especially since Jax is gone. I'm sure he's probably scrambling to try to cover everything."

Myrtle added, "You should just tell him that you hadn't done anything and explain why Jax was lying about you."

Allen set his mouth stubbornly and shook his head. "I'm afraid my pride just won't let me, y'all. The theater and Toucan should have trusted me after all my years of service over there."

He looked sadly down at his empty plate as if he had no idea how it had gone from full to bare. Miles hesitantly asked, "Are you doing all right, Allen? Taking care of yourself and all?"

Allen nodded. "I'm not short on cash, just haven't had it in me to eat. But, sitting here with friends, my appetite came back."

Miles looked a bit glum at having sponsored everyone's lunch as he pulled his wallet out and headed to the front counter to pay.

Myrtle was now eager to be rid of Allen. He appeared to be having so much fun, however, that she worried dumping him was going to prove a chore. All kinds of excuses came to her mind, but in the end, she didn't need any of them since the old boys were still hanging out on the bench in front of the diner. Allen happily greeted them, patted his full tummy, and settled down to gossip.

Myrtle waved him off and then said in a low voice to Miles, "That's just as well. I have other things I want to do today besides hang out with Allen. Want to come with me to the *Bradley Bugle*?"

Miles acquiesced, although going to the newspaper office wasn't very high on his list of things to do.

"And thanks for lunch, Miles. It was delicious, as always. How was your salad?"

Miles sighed. "It was a salad. There's not too much that can go wrong when making a salad, although once I had one that had far too much dressing on it. The big thing is that my stomach doesn't hurt and I don't feel like I'm about to fall asleep in the middle of the day."

"Sounds like a win-win," said Myrtle dryly.

"Uh-oh," muttered Miles.

Myrtle looked up with narrowed eyes to see Eloise beaming at them from across the street and hurrying over.

Chapter Nine

"For heaven's sake," Myrtle grated.

"Hellooo there!" Eloise said cheerily. "Fancy running into the two of you here. I was just thinking about you, Miles, and suddenly my thoughts manifested. It's a miracle."

Myrtle was fairly certain that there was nothing remotely miraculous about the fact that Eloise was stalking Miles. This wasn't the first time since Miles had broken up with Eloise that she'd suddenly appeared. Myrtle was convinced that Eloise suddenly found Miles irresistible because he was no longer available to her. She'd seen it happen all too often in her 80-something years.

Miles gave Eloise a small smile. "Hi there."

"Want to have lunch with me? Both of you are welcome, of course. I thought I'd go to the diner."

Myrtle decided to let Miles handle this all by himself.

Miles cleared his throat. "As a matter of fact, we've already eaten. We're also about to run an errand for Myrtle. Hope you have a nice lunch."

He started hurrying away and Myrtle rushed to keep up with him, her cane thumping on the sidewalk as they scampered off. Myrtle couldn't resist a backward glance and spotted Eloise standing there, watching them go with her hands on her hips. Myrtle chuckled.

"Nicely dispatched, Miles."

Miles looked uncomfortable. "I think I've seen her more now that we're broken up than before."

"Well, even Eloise should get the hint at some point. You're definitely not interested. If she doesn't stop ambushing you like this, you can always call Red and report her as a stalker."

He gave her a wry look. "Thanks, but I think I can handle this."

"If you find that you can't, call him."

The *Bradley Bugle* office was dimly-lit, especially coming off the sunny street. They blinked as their eyes tried to adjust to the lack of light. There was a rustling of papers and a startled, "Miss Myrtle!" from the back of the room, indicating that Myrtle's editor, Sloan, was there. Sloan was a former student of hers and whenever she appeared, he suddenly reverted to being a ninth grader who hadn't completed his homework.

"Sloan?" she called out. Then, in a grumbling voice, "You need to turn on some lights in this place. You'll put your eyes out trying to read in the dark."

There was some crashing around and then, suddenly, light.

"Sorry, Miss Myrtle," said Sloan, looking abashed. "Hi, Miles. Is that better?"

"Somewhat," said Myrtle with a sniff. "I know how it could be even better though. Let me write a piece on Jax's death."

Sloan looked worried. "I've already spoken with Red today. He wanted to keep you out of this one. Said it could get vicious."

"What an extraordinary thing for Red to say! It's already *gotten* vicious, hasn't it? After all, a man is dead and endured a violent death. The circumstances aren't any different than from the other cases I've written about before."

Sloan looked rather miserable at being caught between a rock and a hard place. "I suppose so." He brightened. "Maybe you could do a feature on Jax. You always do wonderful human-interest stories. And it's about time for you to turn in a helpful hints column for me."

Myrtle leveled a stern look at him. "I'm certainly not going to write either one. Not while there's a major story to cover. You know I'm your best crime writer."

Sloan slumped in his chair. "You're my only crime writer. Fortunately, there's not that much crime to speak of."

"Nonsense! There's crime happening all the time. That's what keeps Red gainfully employed."

Miles had been looking curiously at the crossword puzzle that was going to be printed in the paper the following day. He jumped when Myrtle said, "Don't you think so, Miles?"

He nodded vigorously, although he had no idea what Myrtle had just said.

Sloan groaned. "Okay, Miss Myrtle, but try to keep it under your hat. I don't want to end up on the police chief's bad side. Again." He snapped his fingers. "There's something I do need to ask you, though. You know I've been able to make some sense out of Wanda's horoscopes lately. Well, this one has baffled me."

Wanda's horoscopes were eerily accurate, although her lack of general literacy made transcribing them something of a problem.

Sloan handed Myrtle the paper and she peered at it. Miles looked at it over her shoulder.

"What part don't you understand?" asked Myrtle. "It all seems rather self-explanatory to me."

Miles gave her a quizzical look and continued frowning at the hieroglyphics on the paper.

Sloan gestured to the middle of the page. "It sort of goes downhill with Leo. I understand from Aries up until then."

Myrtle grabbed a legal pad and a pen and carefully jotted her transcription in her former teacher handwriting. Then she gave the pad to Sloan.

He nodded. "Okay, this makes a lot more sense." He glanced over the sentences and raised his eyebrows. "Looks like Martha Johnson needs to go to the doctor and get checked out."

Myrtle said, "Sure looks that way. Well, I'd better head on home and start working on the article assignment."

Sloan gave her a glum smile and waved. "See you both later."

Myrtle and Miles walked to his car. "You'd think Sloan would have given up trying to dissuade me from writing crime-related stories. He never wins."

Miles said, "I guess he feels a certain loyalty to Red. Red doesn't want you to write them and Sloan feels the need to try and stop you."

"You'd think *Red* would have given up by now, too," grumbled Myrtle.

Miles made the short drive back to Myrtle's house and then they sat in her driveway for a minute. "What are you planning on doing now?"

"My plans involve watching *Tomorrow's Promise*. Want to join me?"

Miles said, "Sure. I can bring over those puzzle books I was talking about the other day. Maybe we can work on them while we watch."

"Bring the puzzle books, but I can't work on a crossword and watch the show at the same time. This episode is going to require my full concentration."

"Really?" asked Miles. "What did I miss?"

"Nathan is planning on killing Marcus, remember?"

Miles frowned, eyebrows drawing together. "I don't remember that at all."

"Perhaps you were dozing during that part. Marcus discovered Nathan's secret and Nathan is desperate to eliminate Marcus and conceal it."

Miles said, "What was the secret?"

"If you don't know Nathan's secret, Miles, *I'm* certainly not going to be the one to enlighten you. That's why you have to pay attention during the show."

Miles sighed. "That's why I bring my puzzles sometimes. Everything in *Tomorrow's Promise* is very dramatic. I work on puzzles during the parts that are too over-the-top."

"They do call it a soap *opera*. There's nothing more dramatic than opera."

Miles grumbled, "It all seems rather overacted and amateurish."

"That's only because you have a crush on Rowena and she hasn't had much airtime lately."

Miles did return with puzzle books, but the soap that day ended up with a huge Rowena focus so his sudokus fell by the wayside.

The following morning, Myrtle woke up and glanced at the clock. She had the strange sensation she'd overslept, even though it was still very early in the morning.

"Must be because of the service today," she muttered.

She got up and proceeded straight to the kitchen to make a large pot of coffee. She had the feeling she was going to require it. Her conversation with Nicole had made it clear that Jax's memorial service was going to be very unusual indeed.

While she was sitting at the kitchen table making quick work of her crossword puzzle, there was a scratching at the door. Myrtle smiled and opened it to Pasha.

"Brilliant Pasha," she said as she opened a can of cat food.

Pasha gave her what appeared to be a small feline smile as Myrtle placed the food in front of her.

Everything went exactly as it should, smooth as anything. Her crossword was a piece of cake. Her breakfast of granola, yogurt, and banana had been filling and delectable. She pulled out her funeral outfit and, for once, it didn't have a spot on it.

Miles came over at the appointed time to pick her up and she was sitting, ready, in the living room.

"You look rather smug this morning," said Miles with a smile.

"I'm *feeling* very smug. This morning has gone off without a hitch. That's a completely unusual experience for me. Ordinarily, the mornings of funeral services are fraught with pitfalls."

Miles glanced at the clock nervously. "I'm not sure I'd tempt fate, Myrtle. Shouldn't you knock on wood or something?"

Which was precisely when Myrtle, in her previously-spotless funeral outfit, splashed the remainder of her coffee all over herself.

Pasha gave her a dour look. Miles covered his face with his hands.

Myrtle gritted her teeth. "This is going to pose a problem."

"Just find something else to put on. We should be going in a minute or two. You have time to change."

Myrtle hurried to her bedroom, unsure of her choices. She found her old funeral dress in the closet but then realized she didn't have any panty hose. She simply couldn't wear a dress at a funeral service without hose . . . her mother would roll in her grave. Myrtle looked dolefully at the other options in the closet. Her black slacks were in the laundry hamper. The only thing that was suitably dressy were the red slacks that she usually wore for Christmas services. She grimaced. She really needed something more somber to balance them out. She grabbed a black blouse and black shoes and quickly put on the ensemble.

Myrtle grimaced at her reflection. Her hair was standing up like Einstein's. Despite the black blouse and shoes, she still looked entirely too festive. She sighed. It would have to do.

She joined Miles in the living room. He looked slightly surprised at her choice of garments, but was focused on getting them in the car as quickly as possible and to the service.

Miles said, "This is a memorial service, isn't that right?"

"Well, it's a celebration of life. I think that's roughly the same as a memorial service. However, it sounded like this one was going to have a lot of surprises along the way. Nicole said that Jax had left very explicit instructions. I'm not really sure what to expect." Myrtle frowned. "By the way, where are you going?"

Miles blinked. "To the cemetery."

"Well, that's not where the service is. It's in Jax's backyard."

"Really?" This was already bucking tradition. Ordinarily, any type of service was going to be in either the cemetery or the church.

Myrtle nodded. "Take a right here and cut through this neighborhood. We'll save time."

It was evident as soon as they pulled up to Jax's house that everything was going to be very different. There were cars parked all the way up and down the street. Jax's front yard was strung with what appeared to be Christmas lights—the blinking sort.

"Well, Jax was very colorful," said Miles. His voice was doubtful, though.

"I'm just glad that my red slacks fit in better than I thought they would," said Myrtle. She wiggled her nails. "Of course, I guess they don't coordinate very well with my robin's egg blue fingernails, but it's okay."

They walked through the house and into the backyard, which backed up to the lake. There were tables on the sides of the yard fairly groaning with food. There was another long table that was so crowded with hovering people that they couldn't even see what was on it.

"What's over there?" asked Myrtle, craning her head.

Someone moved slightly and Miles raised his eyebrows. "It appears to be an open bar."

"That explains a lot," said Myrtle.

Sure enough, there was a lot of boisterous laughter going on and some back-slapping among Jax's friends. One of them appeared to be singing.

"How long has this service been going on?" asked Myrtle with a frown.

"Perhaps they arrived in that condition," said Miles thoughtfully.

"Just the same, I don't think I'm going to imbibe. There's a limit to how jolly I want to be at a memorial service."

Miles said, "Perhaps it's more acceptable at a celebration of life service."

Several of Jax's friends broke into what sounded like a sea shanty, followed by more hooting laughter.

"No thanks," said Myrtle dryly. "I'll stick with my plan to have *A Mighty Fortress is Our God* at my funeral. Sea shanties, indeed."

There was apparently a funeral director of sorts. A gentleman who was dressed somberly cleared his throat and then announced that the service was about to start and for everyone to take their seats. They all sat in the folding chairs.

"Why do I get the impression that I'm in the audience at the theater?" murmured Myrtle.

Miles said slowly, "Because they've set a stage. Those are props, aren't they?"

They were indeed props. A couple of actors in costume came out and proceeded to work their way through a skit.

Miles was frowning. "Is this—?"

"Yes. It's a spoof of *Waiting for Godot*." Myrtle listened for a few more minutes and said, "A spoof of a spoof, I suppose."

At the end of it, there was scattered applause. Uncertain applause, since everyone was ostensibly at a funeral. The applause became more enthusiastic when Nicole, wearing a flowing, multicolored dress, gave a standing ovation and hooted and hollered in a most dramatic fashion. The performers grinned and bowed.

Next was a soloist. Instead of *A Mighty Fortress is Our God*, the singer sang a selection from what was apparently Jax's favorite show, *Oklahoma!*

Following that, there were a few people who spoke about Jax. The eulogies were relentlessly upbeat and full of humorous stories about Jax's many exploits. Myrtle had the feeling that Nicole had specifically required the eulogists to keep the mood positive.

Nicole went to the front after the last eulogist and said, "That's it, folks. Please fill up your plates with some food. We have all of my dad's favorites, so prepare to have your arteries clogged!"

Myrtle and Miles moved to one of the food tables and saw that it was loaded with fried chicken, biscuits, mac and cheese, baked beans with bacon, hush puppies, fried okra, potato salad, coleslaw, and peach cobbler.

Myrtle said, "Now Miles, you're looking positively queasy again. You're making that same face you make when we go to the diner."

"It's the same food I encounter at the diner," muttered Miles. "Minus the hotdogs."

"Just have some coleslaw and peach cobbler," said Myrtle. She glanced around Jax's backyard. "I've spotted someone we should talk to."

"I certainly hope it's not Eloise." Miles shuddered. "I saw her a little while ago. She winked at me."

"I'm not a bit surprised," said Myrtle darkly. "That's precisely the type of behavior I'd expect from Eloise. Although I do think it takes a lot of audacity to wink at an ex-boyfriend at someone's funeral service, celebration of life or not. And no—Eloise is not on my list to speak with at this event. I want to talk to Bailey."

"Marigold's husband," said Miles.

"That's right. However, I have the feeling Eloise is probably going to hijack you at some point. We just need to make sure we're not sitting with her."

Miles nodded fervently. "Exactly." He turned and glanced around at the different groups of tables and chairs set out. "Looks like Marigold and Bailey are already seated with a couple of drinks at a table."

Myrtle said, "Oh good! Miles, you help me to a plate. Get plenty of food because I might take the extras home for supper."

Miles quirked an eyebrow. "I suppose, at our age, that sort of thing is allowed. Take-out at funerals."

"Of course it is. After all, I blew my budget with my manicure and tipping Jax's daughter. Anyway, I'll go ahead and sit down with them and save you a spot."

Myrtle hurried over to the table where Marigold and Bailey were sitting quietly. She beamed at them. "May Miles and I join you?"

Marigold looked up with relief. "Hi, Miss Myrtle. Yes, please do. I was about to get up and get myself something to eat." And she promptly did just that, delighted at the opportunity to foist Bailey on someone else.

Chapter Ten

Bailey was a rather nerdy-looking fellow. He had a wiry frame, steel-gray hair, and black-framed glasses. He gave Myrtle a tight smile.

Myrtle was glad that Marigold had left because she'd been hoping to speak with Bailey on his own. She was about to launch into her questioning when a voice behind her said, "Hi there, Myrtle! May I squeeze in with you?"

Eloise. Myrtle turned around and snapped, "No, unfortunately, you may not. We're saving these seats for Miles and Marigold."

"But there's plenty of room. I'll just scooch a chair in between these two."

Myrtle had had entirely enough of this. She bared her gritted teeth at Bailey. "I'll be right back. Do save my spot."

"Of course," he said in a rather bemused tone.

Myrtle stood up and grasped Eloise's arm, pulling her out of earshot of others. "Now listen to me and mark my words, Eloise. You are done with stalking Miles. You were unfaithful to him and your relationship is over. He ended it. You clearly have no understanding of what this means, but here it is in a nutshell: you don't see each other anymore socially."

Eloise narrowed her eyes. "You're not the boss of me, Myrtle."

"I'm just letting you know that if you continue hounding Miles, I'll be sure to make your life miserable."

Eloise snorted. "How would you manage to do that?"

"Ask Red. I make his miserable all the time."

Eloise opened her mouth to say something, then thought better of it. Scowling at Myrtle, she slunk away.

Myrtle looked up just in time to see Red quirking an inquiring eyebrow at her from several tables away. She gave him a small smile.

Myrtle rejoined Bailey. "Now then!" she said gaily.

Bailey pushed his glasses up and gave her a small grin. "I'm glad you dodged that one, Miss Myrtle. I wasn't wanting to share a table with Eloise. You might not know it, but she's been spreading rumors that Marigold killed Jax."

"I didn't know it, but I'm certainly not surprised. That's just the type of thing Eloise would do. Now how have you been doing? I haven't seen you around for a while. Been working a lot, I suppose?"

He gave her a solemn look. "Indeed I have, Miss Myrtle. Lots and lots of travel."

Myrtle politely inquired, "What type of work do you do? I can't remember."

"I work in information technology. I sell security software to corporations."

That was decidedly a conversational dead-end since Myrtle knew next to nothing about that. Besides, that wasn't really what she wanted to hear about in the first place. She needed to get information from Bailey before Marigold came back to the table. Fortunately, it appeared that Marigold had no intention of hurrying back over.

"You're not about to retire, then? Spend more time at home?" asked Myrtle.

Bailey pushed his glasses up his nose and regarded Myrtle with that same serious look. "Do you think I should be spending more time at home?"

This question flustered Myrtle a little. "I don't think that's for me to decide."

Bailey said, "I have the feeling you know a bit about Marigold's extracurricular activities."

Myrtle flushed a little. "I might have heard some things. You know how small towns can be."

Bailey nodded. "I was upset when I found out, of course. Marigold and I have been married for a long time. I admit that I've been away from home quite a bit, as you pointed out. The truth of the matter is that I like working and I like the software I'm selling. I also don't really mind traveling to different places and getting a different perspective on the world. It didn't really occur to me that Marigold would be finding someone else to spend time with while I was gone."

He seemed very calm about it all. Myrtle wondered if he'd been this calm when he found out about the affair. He'd said he was "upset." How upset did he get?

"But then, you know how marriage can be," continued Bailey. He paused as if to wait for her to say that she did.

"Sort of," said Myrtle. "My husband died decades ago and my memories are all rather foggy."

"Well, just to remind you, one tends to get in a sort of routine. You build your lives around each other and then you're in this cocoon of habit. I can't really blame Marigold for being lonely and seeking out companionship."

"I think that's very generous of you," said Myrtle.

He shrugged. "Like I said, I was upset at first. But then I thought about it. Jax was pretty much 180 degrees different from me in every way. Where I'm introverted, he was outgoing. Where I love reading, Jax did everything *but* read. Where I'm quiet, Jax was fun and loud."

Myrtle nodded. "Has Red spoken with you? I'm imagining he has."

Bailey said in a tired voice, "Of course he has. I must have looked like the perfect suspect to him. I definitely had motive and I was actually in town when Jax died. But I'd just come back from a trip and my sole focus was spending time with Marigold. And perhaps do some laundry. At any rate, I was home with her and settling back in after being on the road. We had a lovely dinner together at home. I made sure to spend time with her first before recharging my laptop and recording my sales notes for my manager over an email."

It didn't sound like much of an alibi. Marigold could be covering for him or he could have quickly slipped out of the house when he was allegedly composing emails. Myrtle said, "It's nice of you to come to Jax's funeral—considering everything."

Bailey said, "I didn't care about Jax at all, to tell you the truth, although I don't mind sitting here and eating his food and drinking his wine. All I care about is Marigold. Jax wasn't worth going to prison for, as I told your Red. I'm here to support Marigold who *did* care for Jax. It's over now . . . I think it was actually over when I found out about it. And now, after this service, I'm anticipating that everything returns to normal."

Miles, loaded down with food, plopped a plate down in front of her. Myrtle gave him an absent smile. "Bailey, you remember Miles, don't you?"

Bailey's expression indicated that he neither really remembered Miles, nor really cared to. He gave a grunt.

Miles sat down next to Myrtle. Myrtle said, "We were just talking about Jax's death, Miles."

Miles nodded. "Seems an appropriate topic. Considering the circumstances, I mean."

"Yes, I thought so, too." Myrtle noticed that Bailey's gaze was following Marigold sadly around the yard as she spoke with others. "Bailey, do you have any thoughts about who might have done this?"

He brought his attention back to Myrtle with some difficulty. "Done what? This service? His daughter did, I'm sure. Nanette, or whatever her name is."

"Nicole. But I meant Jax's murder. Any guesses on who might have killed him?"

Bailey looked a little bemused at Myrtle's question. Perhaps he wasn't accustomed to octogenarians nosing into murder. "Well . . . no. Why do you ask?"

"Well, I thought you might have heard something from Marigold. Or perhaps you had ideas of your own. If we find out who did it, it would certainly let you off the hook."

Miles sighed. He was used to Myrtle's persistence, but had the feeling that Bailey would like to escape from the table as soon as possible.

"Isn't it usually the spouse?" he asked in a distracted manner.

Myrtle gave him a disappointed look. "Jax was single."

"Oh? I thought Eloise was his wife. I used to see them out and about."

Miles looked deeply unhappy at this.

Myrtle shook her head. "Despite evidence to the contrary, Eloise was not married to Jax."

"I see. Then I really don't know. And I don't really care. Like I said, all I care about is Marigold and making her happy. Things will get back to normal now." It was more of a declaration this time. A notice of intent.

Marigold settled like a butterfly at another table—one populated by some of the more-boisterous male members of the gathering. Bailey quickly stood up. "I'm sorry, but I should join my wife. You'll excuse me, won't you?" Without waiting to find out if they would, he hurried away to her table.

Myrtle said, "Well, I guess that's as much information as I could hope to get from him. What an unusual person he is."

Miles's face indicated that he believed Bailey shared the same opinion about Myrtle. "Did you find out anything from him before I sat down?"

"I suppose so. Nothing earth-shattering. He thinks Marigold just needed a change of pace and that's why she embarked on a relationship with Jax. Bailey said Jax was completely different from him."

"Very true," said Miles. "But I can't imagine he was as calm about it as you're making him sound."

"That's the thing—he *was* calm about it. He acknowledged that he'd 'been upset' when he'd discovered Marigold was cheating on him, but seems very matter-of-fact about it now. He also gave something of an alibi, although it relies on Marigold. He was at home spending time with her when Jax was killed."

"And here he is at his rival's funeral," said Miles.

"Yes, but he said that was because he was trying to be supportive of Marigold. He said he didn't care anything about Jax. Why would he?"

Miles ate some of his coleslaw and then swallowed. "I thought I spotted you yelling at Eloise."

"Don't be silly. I don't yell at people."

"You had that look on your face that said you meant business," said Miles.

Myrtle sniffed. "It's better to be direct with some people."

"Should I ask what was discussed?"

"I think not. I'm just hoping that will be the end of that. It just depends on how much sense Eloise has. I'm starting to suspect she doesn't have much."

The rest of the celebration of life service and, indeed, the following day went very quietly for Myrtle. Her article was published in the newspaper and Red was apparently too busy hunting down bad guys to call her or be grouchy about it. She happily ate the different baked concoctions that Miles's well-meaning women friends brought over to him (and which he quickly delivered over to her).

Even after eating wonderful baked goods (or, perhaps, because of all the carbs sitting like a rock in her tummy), Myrtle had a very difficult time sleeping that night. Finally, around two a.m., Myrtle decided she might as well get up. She puttered around the house a little, but couldn't seem to focus on anything—not her puzzle book, not the television, not the book she was reading. She decided finally to walk through her backyard and out the gate and down to the sloping path to the lake. Sitting in the rocking chair on her dock and looking out on the water could be soothing.

And indeed, it started that way. The moon wasn't full, but it was full enough to spill light on the water as it lapped against the dock. The frogs were singing to each other and she could hear crickets chirping, too. Lightning bugs were lighting up here and there as they looked for a mate. The only thing that seemed to break the peaceful vista was a lump in the water. Myrtle really wished people would stop dumping their yard waste into the lake. It was incredibly lazy of them to just chuck it into the water and made for hazards on the lake.

As she looked more closely at the lump, Myrtle wondered what sort of trash it was. It looked almost like part of a log. But then, Myrtle realized it wasn't part of a log at all—it was a person.

Chapter Eleven

Cursing the fact that she'd neglected to put her phone in her robe pocket, Myrtle hurried back up the path, leaning heavily on her cane as she went. She pushed through her back door and into her kitchen, grabbing her phone.

Red's number rang so many times that Myrtle thought it would end up going to voice mail. Finally, he picked up. "Mama," he said gruffly. "Are you okay?"

"No, I'm not okay. Well, I'm okay, but I'm not really."

Red was starting to sound a little more alert. "Chest pains? Or did you fall down."

"Don't be silly. I'm completely fine. Better, at any rate, than the body I just saw floating in the lake behind my house."

Red now was entirely awake. "I'll be right there," he said shortly before hanging up.

Myrtle was now even more restless than she'd been when she'd wandered out to the dock to begin with. She decided to make a large pot of coffee since Red would soon be there and seemed like he might be able to use some caffeine. When there was a tap on the front door, she hurried to open it. But it was Miles.

"I couldn't sleep and saw your light on," he said. He sniffed the air and said, "Seems like you've already made coffee."

"Yes, come on in. I thought you were Red."

Miles raised his eyebrows. "You were expecting Red? At two a.m.?"

"Yes. I called him. There's a body in the lake behind my house."

Miles just stared at her.

"It does look as if you could use some coffee, Miles. Here, let's make you a cup."

While she was doing that, Red opened the front door and came right on in. He didn't seem at all surprised to see Miles there and bobbed his head in greeting to him. "Was it just directly out the back?" he asked.

"Straight ahead, unless the water has moved it along. You'll take the boat, won't you?" asked Myrtle.

It was Red's boat—he'd bought it from her years ago. But his house didn't back up to the water like Myrtle's did.

He shook his head and said in a somewhat distracted voice, "My deputy is getting the police watercraft out. It shouldn't be a personal boat for a recovery effort."

Red walked out and down to the dock as Myrtle and Miles watched him from the back window.

Without much time passing at all, the police watercraft, well-lit and moving slowly, approached Myrtle's dock. Red was on the dock, directing his deputy and the other men who were aboard.

"Must be the state police with the deputy," said Myrtle. "I suppose they're staying here in town for a few days." She frowned at Miles who was pacing a bit from window to back door to window. "For heaven's sake, Miles, do you have ants in your pants? I've never seen you so restless."

He sighed. "I just have a bad feeling about this."

"You're starting to sound like your cousin Wanda. Next thing we know, you'll be palm reading."

Miles kept looking out the window.

"Look, it's going to take a while for them to recover the body. Besides, Red is unlikely to give us any information at all. Let's do something while we wait."

Miles said gloomily, "Wait for what? You just said that Red isn't going to provide us with any information."

"That doesn't mean that I'm not going to try," said Myrtle. "I should be able to get *something*, if not from him than from Lieutenant Perkins. In the meantime, we'll play canasta."

Miles muttered, "Canasta for two people is sort of a pain."

"We'll get fifteen cards apiece and it will be just fine," said Myrtle with a determined edge to her voice.

They started playing, Miles desolately going through the motions of drawing and discarding cards. There was another rap at Myrtle's door.

"This place is absurd," said Myrtle. "I get more foot traffic through my house than an airport does."

It was Wanda at the door, looking tired, but giving her a big gap-toothed smile.

"Wanda!" said Myrtle. "Miles and I were just talking about you. You didn't *walk* here again, did you?"

Wanda shook her head. "Made Dan take me. Took a while to git one of the cars started."

Myrtle supposed the backfiring noise she heard from the street was Dan's unsubtle departure.

"Come on in," said Myrtle, bustling back to the kitchen. Wanda looked at the cards in fascination. Myrtle had introduced her to card games recently and Wanda had quickly taken to them. "Maybe you can take my spot in the game after we get you a snack and some coffee. I need to make another pot."

Miles said, "Wanda can take my spot. I wasn't playing very well anyway."

"No, no. The whole reason we were playing cards to begin with is so you could be distracted," said Myrtle briskly.

Wanda said, "From the body in the lake." She gave Miles and Myrtle a knowing look.

Miles shivered. He was never fond of Wanda's eerie gift.

"I figured you probably knew all about it," said Myrtle. She paused. "What can you tell us?"

Wanda said in her cigarette-ruined, grating voice, "Miles is gonna get some questions."

Miles promptly turned pale. He said, stammering a little, "Is it Eloise?"

Wanda gave him a nod, looking very serious.

Miles slumped in his chair. "Oh no."

Myrtle hurried back into the kitchen and found her bottle of sherry. She poured Miles a generous amount, forgoing her dainty sherry glasses and choosing a regular water glass, and thrust it at him.

He looked glumly at the sherry before taking a small sip.

Myrtle said in a stern voice, "You're going to need to take a gulp of it, Miles. I want to see your color come back."

He took a bigger sip, coughed a little, but ultimately looked more like himself. "There now. That's better." Myrtle turned to Wanda. "What else do you know about this? I know Red's not going to tell me much."

Wanda shook her head. "Not much. Just that she's been murdered."

"So she wasn't out for a night swim that went horribly wrong," said Myrtle. "Not that I really supposed she had."

Miles moaned. "They think I did it."

Myrtle frowned at him. "Drink your sherry. No one who knows you thinks that. Besides, I told Eloise to leave you alone."

Wanda grated, "Yer gonna git questions, too."

"Well, I gathered that. And that's not to say I wasn't angry with Eloise. She made me furious, chasing poor Miles around."

Miles gave another moan and Myrtle gave him an irritated look. "Sherry, Miles. You're going to be just fine. Thanks to me, you haven't even been around Eloise since before Jax's service."

Miles shook his head miserably. "That's not entirely true. Eloise showed up at my house earlier tonight."

Myrtle put her hands on her hips. "That scamp!"

Miles sighed. "I thought I was handling it all very well. I didn't let Eloise force her way into the house like she usually did. I stood on the doorstep and told her very firmly that our relationship was over and that I believed we needed to spend some time apart from each other. Then, perhaps as time passed, we'd be able to at least be friendly again."

Myrtle snorted. "I can only imagine how she took that."

Miles nodded. "She was very animated as a result."

Wanda said in a faraway tone. "An' Red saw it."

"*Red* saw it? Oh no. No wonder you're going to get some questions, Miles."

Miles said, "He was getting out of his car across the street when it happened. Eloise was upset and stormed off. Red watched her drive off. I think he had half a mind to pull her over because she was driving way too fast in the neighborhood."

Myrtle's back door opened and they hushed up as a serious-looking Red came in. Again, he didn't seem surprised at all by seeing an additional person at Myrtle's. "Hi there, Wanda," he said vaguely.

Wanda gave him a smile.

Red said gruffly, "Now Mama, I realize from your display out on the front lawn that you haven't been happy about me asking Miles questions."

Myrtle sniffed.

"But I can't show any favoritism with a murder investigation. You understand that, don't you?"

Myrtle narrowed her eyes at him and refused to answer.

He sighed and turned apologetically to Miles. "Eloise was the body in the lake, I'm afraid."

"Wanda has already informed us of that," said Myrtle coolly.

Red gave Wanda a suspicious look.

Myrtle said, "And Red, you'll have to do something about Bingo."

Red frowned at his mother.

"Eloise's dog. I'm sure it's probably alone in her house now."

Red said, "We'll have someone take him over to the station. Maybe some of Eloise's family will want him. Now Miles. I wanted to ask you a few questions about your argument with

Eloise earlier tonight. Of course I know the two of you were dating."

Miles sighed. "I'm afraid we had been."

Red took out his small notebook and made a note with an equally small pencil. "And that relationship came to an end, you'd said."

Myrtle gave a snort and Red frowned at her. "You have a comment about that, Mama?"

"I do. Miles, who is always the perfect gentleman, ended the relationship. Eloise apparently had no clue how to behave as an ex-girlfriend, so she continued chasing Miles. It was quite ridiculous and appalling. I was going to report her for stalking Miles at one point."

Wanda piped up in her grating voice. "She was tryin' to win him back."

Miles looked miserably down at his hands.

Red said politely, "Well, Miles is quite a catch. So is that what was going on earlier tonight, then? Eloise came over to your house and tried to talk you into continuing your relationship?"

Miles nodded. "I'd actually already turned in for the night and heard my doorbell ring, which woke me up. And it was a bit startling, too."

Red quirked an eyebrow. "Is it? I was under the impression that my mother frequently goes over to your house at odd hours and rings your doorbell. Didn't you just assume it was her?"

Miles said, "Myrtle usually knocks. And, most of the time, she does look to see if there's a light on or not. *Most* of the time."

Myrtle blushed. Sometimes she forgot. Or sometimes it didn't really seem all that important for Miles to be awake because she had something important on her mind.

"I do usually knock," she said simply.

Red gave her a skeptical look. "Okay. So your doorbell rang, Miles, and you woke up and felt startled. You proceeded to answer the door and you saw Eloise there. I'm guessing you weren't too delighted to see her."

Myrtle said, "Not upset enough to drown her in the lake, though."

Miles paled a little, whether at the mention of a dead Eloise or at the idea of him drowning someone, it wasn't entirely clear.

"No one has mentioned anything about Eloise being drowned in the lake," said Red severely.

"We're not stupid, Red," said Myrtle regally. "And there's something you should know about Eloise's swimming ability. Or lack of it."

She looked at Miles and he said, "Eloise couldn't swim. It was something she was embarrassed about so she didn't tell anyone."

Red rubbed the side of his head as if something was throbbing there. "All right. Good to know, although it's too bad that just the two of you know that little fact. Now, you were upset with Eloise, Miles. And that's completely understandable. It must be very frustrating to politely end a relationship with someone only to have them constantly trying to reignite something."

Myrtle snorted again. "I don't think the 'relationship' was ignited to begin with. The problem was with Eloise. She was being unreasonable and pushy and needed to leave Miles alone."

Red looked very tired. "This leads me to something else I needed to bring up. Mama, I saw you have a run-in with Eloise at Jax's service."

"Well, naturally. If you'd been doing your job at all, you'd have noticed that. I wasn't trying to be subtle because Eloise was the type of person who was completely immune to subtlety. Pasha couldn't stand her," said Myrtle as if that settled everything.

Red closed his eyes briefly. "Okay. What did you say to Eloise?"

"What do you think? I said I could make her life very difficult for her if she didn't leave Miles alone."

Miles shifted uncomfortably in his chair.

Wanda said, "She didn't have nuthin' to do with this."

Red said, "Oh, that I know. Mama is a rascal, but she doesn't go drown folks."

Miles turned slightly green and Red said, "Sorry, Miles."

"More sherry?" asked Myrtle.

Miles shook his head.

Red continued, "You see my dilemma though, don't you? Both of y'all had words with Eloise. Mama, you directly threatened her. And now she's gone. It's not a very good situation to be in. I need you both to think very carefully about your involvement in this case and make sure you back off. The last thing you need is to be hauled in officially for questioning by the state police."

Myrtle said coldly, "Lieutenant Perkins has entirely too much sense to do such a thing. And now, Red, if you're done upsetting us, we have a game of canasta to play."

Red stood up. "Just remember what I said." With that stern advice, he took his leave.

Miles said, "Well, that officially stressed me out."

Wanda croaked, "You'll be okay."

Miles gave her a hopeful look as if he wasn't entirely prepared to believe her, but very much wanted to.

Myrtle got up and briskly moved to the kitchen. "Let's just bring the sherry bottle out here in the living room."

Miles said glumly, "I doubt that will help with my canasta-playing skills."

Wanda turned Myrtle down for alcohol, but Miles did take a bit more of the sherry, although it wasn't his favorite beverage to imbibe. Myrtle poured herself a very tiny glass and took a delicate sip of it.

"What are we going to do?" asked Miles.

"Do?" asked Myrtle. "We're going to clear our names and solve this case."

Now Miles looked rather panicky. "Myrtle, we were just told to back off and not have anything to do with this case. So . . . I think we should back off and not have anything to do with this case."

Myrtle snorted. "No, we should do precisely the opposite. Do you want to leave our fates up to Red? Absolutely not. Tomorrow we start digging to find out who killed Eloise. I guarantee you that whoever did also killed Jax and is trying to cover their tracks." She turned to Wanda. "Wanda, do you have any thoughts about this case?"

Wanda said sadly, "Not real clear thoughts. Something about Sherry."

Myrtle's gaze dropped to the glasses in front of them. "Sherry?"

Wanda shook her head. "Not that kind of sherry. A person."

Myrtle and Miles looked at each other. "Sherry, our neighbor," said Myrtle. "Although how she figures in is anybody's guess. Did she even really know Jax or Eloise?"

Miles said, "Sherry definitely knows Eloise. They went to the movies together from time to time. I was always glad that Sherry wanted to go out when I didn't want to."

"Well, it sounds like we'll have to add Sherry to our list of people to talk to."

"An' tea."

"Tea. Interesting. Tea has already figured into this investigation. I shall have to mull on that." Then Myrtle gave Miles a critical look. "You still look sort of peaked, Miles. Go ahead and play canasta with Wanda—it will be good for you."

So while Miles and Wanda played cards, Myrtle made a list of names and little notes beside each one. She listed all the suspects and ranked them.

After Miles and Wanda were done and Wanda declared the winner, Myrtle said, "All right, I think I have a plan to execute."

Miles winced. "Let's not use the word *execute* right now."

"Fine. I have a plan of action for us starting tomorrow. We'll go around and see as many suspects as we possibly can as soon as we can squeeze them in. So, to recap, that's Bailey Pratt and his wife Marigold; Allen West, formerly with the theater; and Jax's daughter Nicole."

"And me," said Miles glumly.

Myrtle rolled her eyes. "Snap out of it, Miles. If you're on that list, then I'd have to be too since I was harassing Eloise at Jax's service. We're going to speak with these folks and then we're going to put all the pieces together. We don't have any time to spare."

Miles looked alarmed. "We're not going out to speak with anyone now, are we? It's nearly three o'clock in the morning. They'll be calling the police on us."

"No. Now we're going to go to sleep to prepare for our big day today. Wanda, you can take my guest room."

Miles left and Myrtle locked the door behind him then brought Wanda a new toothbrush and an extra blanket. Then, finally, Myrtle turned in and fell right to sleep . . . a most unusual occurrence.

Chapter Twelve

When she woke up later, it was to the sound of thunder cracking overhead. Myrtle groaned. Apparently, the weather hadn't gotten the memo that they were going to be out and about a lot today.

Wanda was still sleeping, so Myrtle tried to be quiet as she got ready. She pulled out her big umbrella to get the paper at the end of her driveway since it was now raining buckets. Lightning flashed overhead as she returned with the paper and she jumped as something brushed against her leg.

"Pasha! Oh, poor baby. Here, come inside."

Pasha eagerly followed her in. Pasha, as a feral cat, was accustomed to all sorts of weather, but this was some of the worst. At least the cat was good about letting Myrtle know when she wanted to be indoors for a while.

Myrtle dug out an old towel and carefully wiped Pasha down. Then she got her a can of cat food, which Pasha quickly devoured. As Myrtle solved the daily crossword, Pasha sat in the window watching the storm outside with interest.

A particularly loud clap of thunder made both Myrtle and Pasha jump and even woke the deep-sleeping Wanda from her slumbers. Wanda wandered sleepily out of the guest room and Pasha bounded happily over to see her. It was unusual for Pasha to take to people, but Wanda and the black cat always got along perfectly.

Myrtle beamed at Wanda and Pasha and said, "I'll make us some breakfast."

Wanda shook her head though. "Nope. *I'll* make us breakfast. You just do yer puzzle."

Myrtle remembered that, once before, Wanda had cooked a marvelous and extravagant breakfast for her. "Thank you, Wanda," she said instead.

Wanda was very adept in the kitchen. She made eggs and bacon, cheese grits and toast with jam.

"Wanda, this is fabulous," said Myrtle after taking a big bite.

Wanda gave her a shy smile.

After breakfast, Myrtle called Miles. "Ready to unmask the murderer?"

"I wasn't aware it was a masked bandit," said Miles. "And no, I'm still not entirely sure this is a good idea. It makes me look like I'm in more trouble than I am."

Myrtle said, "As far as we know, we're both in a lot of trouble. You and I both had words with Eloise, witnessed by others. We've got to get to the bottom of this now."

Wanda croaked from behind her, "I can go with you, Myrtle."

Miles heard her over the phone and eagerly said, "Yes, Wanda's a better fit for today."

Myrtle tapped her foot impatiently. It was so aggravating when Miles was difficult. Ordinarily, he was happy to cooperate.

"Okay, here's the plan. Wanda will go with me to see our first interviewees of the day, Bailey and Marigold. That will give you some time to mope around the house, Miles, which is apparently what you're wanting to do. Have some coffee, watch some mindless TV, then you can come with me to talk to the next of our suspects."

Miles sighed. "I suppose so."

"Good. I'll call you in a little while." Myrtle hung up the phone and clicked her tongue in annoyance.

Wanda drawled, "He's just worried. Prob'ly upset his tummy."

"Oh, I'd forgotten what happens with his stomach when he's stressed. Yes, you're probably right. Well then, it's just as well that he's not with us right now."

Wanda gave Myrtle a thoughtful look. "How're you gonna git in to see them people?"

"You mean Bailey and Marigold? I'll just tell them we were walking by and I wanted a glass of water. When you're my age, people just let you in their house. They don't want anyone to expire on their front step."

"And me?" asked Wanda.

Myrtle made a dismissive gesture with her hand. "Everyone is fascinated by you, Wanda. They'll want you to read their palms and tell them what's coming down the line for them."

Wanda looked grim. "Sometimes what's comin' down the line ain't good. Then they get upset."

"I would imagine that would be quite the occupational hazard. Let's just see how it goes."

As it happened, Bailey and Marigold's house was a fair distance from Myrtle's house on Magnolia Lane. By the time she reached it, she was indeed thirsty and Wanda was, too.

Myrtle walked right up to their front door and tapped loudly. Then she stood back, leaning heavily on her cane and looking as frail as a tall, large-boned lady was able to look.

The door opened and Bailey stood there, looking rather startled at the sudden appearance of an octogenarian and a psychic on his front porch.

"Miss Myrtle!" he said with concern. "Is something wrong?"

Myrtle gave him a weak smile and said faintly, "I'm rather parched, Bailey. Wanda and I were taking a stroll and I suddenly felt as if I were having a spell."

Bailey's already wide eyes opened even wider. He appeared to have no idea what a spell might encompass, but he was positive he didn't want Myrtle to have one outside his front door. "Here, come inside," he said, ushering Myrtle in. Wanda lingered uncomfortably in the back and he prompted, "And you, too, uh . . . Wanda."

Bailey gestured to chairs in the living room and hurried off to get the water. Myrtle looked around them. The living room was quite grand with a collection of fine antiques and paintings. Myrtle sat up a little straighter than usual.

"Nice place," grated Wanda.

"Yes indeed," said Myrtle. Then she added in a hushed tone, "But not very comfortable, is it?"

Wanda shook her head in agreement.

Bailey returned with the ice waters for both Myrtle and Wanda and they took a couple of big gulps.

Myrtle gave him a smile. "You're a lifesaver."

Bailey became flustered. "I'm not sure about that, Miss Myrtle. Do I need to call an ambulance? You mentioned having a spell."

"Oh no, no. I'm just fine now. I suppose I must have gotten dehydrated. Dehydration does terrible things to a body."

Bailey glanced at his watch. "Marigold should be coming back any minute now. I'm about to have to go run to a meeting for my work."

Myrtle gave him an innocent, feeble look. "Should Wanda and I go then?"

"I don't really think that's a good idea, Miss Myrtle. You're only just now getting your color back."

Myrtle was surprised to hear that she had lost or gained color. Her coloring always seemed rather status quo to her.

Bailey continued, "I think you should stay here after Marigold comes in, just to be sure. Then she can drive you back home." He hesitated. "I suppose I can talk for a few minutes before I have to leave. I don't want to be a bad host."

Myrtle said, "Well, that would be lovely. I'd like a little mini-visit, wouldn't you, Wanda?"

Wanda silently nodded.

Bailey cleared his throat. "All right then. Let's see." He seemed to be searching his mind for some sort of topic that would be suitable for his unusual visitors. He finally seized on: "What's new with you?"

Little did Bailey realize the can of worms he was opening up. Myrtle beamed at him. "Actually, I had quite a night last night. Wouldn't you agree, Wanda?"

Wanda croaked, "It was somethin' else."

Bailey gave them a polite smile in return. "Really? What was it—a lost dog? A boy setting off firecrackers?" He frowned, wondering if there was a recurring pattern. "Nothing medical, I hope." His gaze flicked over to his cell phone as if he was still contemplating a 911 call.

Myrtle did so hate to be patronized. She said with a bit of bite in her voice, "No. I discovered a dead body."

Now *Bailey* was the one who lost color. "What's that?"

Myrtle looked across at Wanda. "It's hard to believe word hasn't gotten out about that yet. I guess that's what happens when bodies are discovered late at night."

"Guess so," said Wanda, agreeably.

Bailey said, "Where was the body? And who was it? Did you call the police?"

Myrtle pressed her lips together. She had the feeling that Bailey thought her somewhat incompetent. In her school-teacher voice she said, "The body was floating in the lake behind my house. Of *course* I called the police. The chief of police and I are fairly close, as you know."

Bailey looked chastened. "Sorry, I forget that sometimes. I don't often see you and Red together."

Myrtle sniffed. "That's by design. And to answer your last question, it was Eloise Pembroke."

"Eloise." Bailey sat back in his chair, looking suddenly exhausted. Then he rallied for a second. "You just had an argument with Eloise at Jax's service. I heard you."

Myrtle's expression was frosty. "That was my attempt at keeping Eloise in line. However, she didn't seem to heed it."

"An' now she's dead," said Wanda in a laconic voice.

Bailey pressed his hands up against his face.

"Where were the two of you last night?" asked Myrtle sweetly.

Bailey stammered, "Not out drowning anyone."

Myrtle waited for a better explanation, letting the seconds tick by while she drank the rest of her water.

Bailey, finally not able to stand the silence, said, "Marigold and I were here together last night, of course."

Myrtle clicked her tongue. "There's something about your demeanor that isn't very believable, Bailey."

Wanda croaked, "You weren't here."

Myrtle said sternly to Bailey, "When you have a psychic telling you that you weren't here, that's a bad sign."

Bailey's shoulders slumped. "Miss Myrtle, you should go ahead and call Red. I want to confess."

Myrtle stared at him. Then she and Wanda stared at each other.

Wanda said, "I ain't said you was out killin' nobody. Jest said you wasn't home."

Bailey shrugged. "Regardless, I did it. I killed Eloise."

Myrtle said flatly, "And Jax."

"Yes, that's right. Jax, too. So call Red and get him over here."

Myrtle frowned and pulled her old schoolteacher voice back into service. "Now Bailey, Red's not much of a fan of getting his time wasted, especially in the middle of a murder investigation. Are you absolutely certain that you're responsible for two deaths? Why don't you walk us through them?"

Bailey froze as if he had been given a pop quiz. "Well, I was upset with Jax, of course. You know why I was. It's perfectly understandable that I would want to kill him for having an affair with Marigold."

Myrtle said, "Wanting to kill someone and actually following through with it are two entirely different things."

"Yes. But I did. I went over to Jax's house and I did."

"Hm," said Myrtle. "And Eloise? Because you seemed genuinely surprised a few minutes ago when I mentioned her body was found in the lake."

"Yes, well, I drowned her. She knew I'd killed Jax and she was harassing me about it," said Bailey. He looked pleased that he'd landed on a viable explanation for killing Eloise.

Myrtle and Wanda stared at each other again. Wanda shook her head.

"I'll call Red, Bailey. But I don't think you're telling the truth." Myrtle took her phone out of her enormous purse and punched Red's number in. "Red?"

There was a groan on the other end of the phone. "What now, Mama?"

"What a terrible way to greet one's mother. I'm simply calling to let you know that Bailey Pratt has just confessed to killing Jax. And, as an afterthought, Eloise, too. We're at Bailey's house."

Red suddenly sounded very much on edge. "Mama, you're not alone with Bailey, are you?"

"Heavens, no. I have Wanda here with me."

"I'll be right there," said Red grimly.

And he was. Minutes later, he and the state police arrived and ushered Myrtle and Wanda out of the house.

Which was precisely when Marigold showed up, looking bewildered at the number of police vehicles in her driveway.

Chapter Thirteen

"What's going on?" she gasped as she hurried over to Myrtle and Wanda.

Myrtle and Wanda were sitting on a bench under a tree in Marigold's well-landscaped front yard. "Bailey confessed to killing Jax and Eloise."

Marigold suddenly looked extremely annoyed. "He did *what*?" She shook her head and stared at the house with fury in her eyes.

Myrtle said mildly, "Wanda and I don't think he did it."

"Of *course* he didn't do it. Oh, this is completely absurd."

Myrtle said, "Would you like to take a seat, dear?" There was another bench facing Myrtle and Wanda. It was quite a large yard.

Marigold sighed. "I guess I can't go inside right now. Not with the police here and everything. What a silly mess." She rubbed her forehead as if it hurt. "And now he can't give *me* an alibi because he says he was out."

"*Was* he out?" asked Myrtle. "Wanda seemed to think so."

Wanda looked steadily at Marigold.

Marigold sighed again. "He was out drinking. I guess he wouldn't have been able to give me much of an alibi anyway. We'd had an argument, which was unusual since we rarely have them. But now Bailey is more on edge. He thinks now that Jax is out of the way, our lives should just fall right back into our routine again."

Myrtle tilted her head to one side. "But you don't think that can happen, do you?"

Marigold shook her head. "No. I'm sure that we can't. Too much has changed between us. Or maybe, too much has changed with just me. I'm not the same person I was when we married."

"I'm guessing that if you don't see a way for the two of you to pick back up again, that you're planning on leaving Bailey."

"I'm afraid so. I don't have anything against Bailey—he's always been very kind to me and he's been a good provider. But I just can't go on like this. I really feel like I'm living just half a life. At this point, I want to have an amicable parting of the ways and find someone more compatible for me before it's too late."

Myrtle felt very much like she'd just been dropped into an episode of *Tomorrow's Promise*. Except, perhaps the script wasn't quite as smooth. Still, she gave Marigold an encouraging nod. And wondered, as Marigold looked away, if she'd already found that more-compatible companion.

Marigold turned her attention to Wanda, who was still regarding her with that steady expression. She gave Wanda a quick smile. "Do you see a future for me? I mean, I don't know how it all works, but can you see what's going to happen to me?"

Wanda looked uncomfortable. "That's not really how the sight works."

Myrtle said, "I've learned the sight is very ornery and plays by its own rules, Marigold."

Marigold leaned eagerly toward the psychic. "How about general feelings in regard to me? Hopeful? Sad?"

Wanda shook her head regretfully.

Myrtle stepped in before Marigold could continue pressing Wanda for information. "What did you think when you heard about Eloise's death, Marigold?"

"Well, I heard about it over at the library a few minutes ago and I was very surprised . . . and a little worried. I started wondering if it's safe to walk around downtown alone. You know, if there's a killer wandering around. I'm starting to wonder if it isn't just someone killing random people. Someone who's really deranged."

Myrtle thought that sounded like a lot of wistful nonsense but she said, "I suppose it could be. You never know these days, do you? But if it *isn't* a deranged stranger, who do you think might have been responsible for these deaths?"

Marigold looked thoughtful. "I hadn't thought much about it until the last day or so, but I've heard that Allen West remains really bitter about Jax's role in Allen getting kicked out of his job at the theater."

"It wasn't a paying job," said Myrtle in the tone of someone wanting to set the record straight.

"No? I guess that was generous of him to volunteer," said Marigold, sounding doubtful. "The thing is, Jax had a real problem with Allen. The more I think about it, the more I'm sure Allen had something to do with all this."

Myrtle said, "What do you remember about their interactions with each other?"

Marigold sighed. "Well, at first I didn't remember a whole lot because I'd kind of brushed it off as drama. Honestly, it was sort of like drama between high school girls. I wasn't interested in it or listening to Jax complain about Allen. But basically, Jax and I stepped out of his house recently to head to the movies and Jax's tire was slashed."

Myrtle said, "And you thought Allen had done it?"

"I didn't think *anything* because I was a disinterested bystander, like I said. But *Jax* definitely thought Allen was behind it. He said it was exactly the kind of passive-aggressive thing Allen would do to indicate his displeasure."

Wanda croaked, "You think Allen killed Jax an' Eloise?"

Marigold shrugged. "Why not? He was clearly unhappy with Jax. And maybe Eloise knew something and Allen had to get rid of her, too. It all fits together. When Red comes back outside, I'm going to tell him all about it."

As if on cue, Red walked outside of the house, a grim look on his face. Myrtle noted that he did *not* have Bailey with him in handcuffs. He sighed as he spotted his mother and Wanda there with Marigold. Marigold waved him over.

Marigold said to Red, "I'm guessing you realize Bailey's confession is totally ridiculous."

Red said in that cautious way of his, "Let's just say there are too many inconsistencies in his story. Because his account isn't credible, we won't be taking him in." He paused. "Marigold, do you have any idea why Bailey might confess to something he didn't do?"

Marigold's expression was quite displeased. She pursed her lips. "I can only imagine that it was an ill-conceived plan to protect me from being a suspect."

Red said, "So he thought you might be responsible?"

Marigold said, "I suppose he thought it was a possibility since he hasn't been around enough to know where I've been at different times of the day. And that's one of the most annoying things—if Bailey *had* been home, he'd have been able to provide me with an alibi. Because I've been here."

Red nodded. "I gathered that Bailey was out at the approximate time of both of the deaths."

Myrtle noticed that Marigold didn't seem to be in any hurry to lie for Bailey's sake, unlike Bailey's selfless confession.

"That's right. He likes to go for drives," said Marigold, rolling her eyes. "And he likes to go out drinking, too. Perhaps one of the regulars can give him an alibi." Then she said, "There was something I thought you should know about a possible suspect."

Red hastily interjected, "Got it. Let's meet inside, please. I'll be right there."

Marigold walked into the house and Red said, "Now, Mama. This is really getting silly. You're turning up all over the place."

Myrtle sniffed. "That's because you're treating Miles and me like suspects. Naturally, we're going to want to clear our names. Don't be silly. And it's pointless to try to hide information from us, by the way. Marigold already told Wanda and me all about her 'possible suspect.'"

Red rubbed his eyes with the heels of his hands. "Fine. But this needs to stop here, Mama. You're getting too involved. You're showing up all over town, talking to too many people and being too nosy. You're going to end up getting yourself into hot water." He looked at Wanda, who was sitting with her hands politely folded in her lap. "Wanda, you seem like you have a lot of common sense. Can you figure out some sort of diversion for my mother that doesn't seem to involve murder?" He snapped his fingers. "I know. Christy Heatherington needs a visit."

Myrtle said, "Perhaps she does. But I don't believe Christy needs a visit from *me*."

"She's at Greener Pastures, of course, and was talking about petitioning the administration to make a few changes over there," said Red in a wheedling voice.

Myrtle stared at him. "You're actually encouraging me to create another insurrection at that retirement facility?"

"I don't think Christy used the term *insurrection*, but she'd like some ideas on how to implement changes," said Red.

Myrtle said flatly, "This reinforces the fact that you're completely desperate. Do you really believe I'm in danger? Wanda isn't even saying I'm in danger and she *always* does."

Wanda looked at Myrtle seriously. "Yer in danger."

Myrtle sighed. "Okay. But you know how the sight works for Wanda. It's very vague. I could technically be in terrible danger from a staircase or faulty wiring or a defective airbag in Miles's car."

Red drawled, "Considering you're dabbling in a murder case, I'd guess the danger is something very different." One of the state police officers called out to Red and he quickly grunted out a goodbye and stalked off.

Myrtle and Wanda started on their long walk back to Myrtle's house.

"Sorry," said Wanda. "Shouldn't have told Red that."

"It doesn't really matter since Red *always* thinks I'm in danger, anyway. He things I'm grossly incompetent at being an adult, although I've been an adult for the last 60-odd years of my life." Myrtle looked curiously at Wanda. "You were really shutting down Marigold's request for a fortune. Are you feeling worn out? I know psychic activity can be wearing for you."

Wanda looked a little uncomfortable. "Nothin' like that. Just had a bad feelin'. When folks ask for their future, they want to hear the good stuff. Didn't see nothin' good for her." She shrugged her thin shoulders.

"Well, I can understand where you wouldn't want to be the bearer of bad news. I can't say I find Marigold a particularly sympathetic character, but it's too bad she has troubles heading her way." Myrtle's expression darkened as her thoughts moved back to Red. "I know what will get Red's goat. I need to write a story for the paper on Eloise's death. Since I was practically an eyewitness, that should make for good copy."

Wanda gave her a wary look. "Just remember . . . yer in danger."

"I promise I won't advertise who the killer is. Mainly because I don't know yet." Myrtle sighed. "It does all make Miles and me look rather guilty, though, doesn't it? That Eloise! She was constantly causing trouble and has apparently decided to continue from beyond the grave."

Finally back at Myrtle's house, they walked inside and Myrtle poured them some lemonade. "Now, when Miles comes over, he and I'll head over to see Allen. Maybe you can hang out here, Wanda, and watch *Tomorrow's Promise*. Do you have any insights at all on Allen?"

Wanda said, "Needs to start clippin' coupons."

"Hm. So Allen is facing some financial issues. I wonder if that means something."

Wanda drawled, "Means he's spendin' too much cash."

Myrtle sighed. "And that's all it might mean, sure enough. I'm running fairly low on cash, myself. Thank heaven Miles has been the recipient of so much food from the good widows of Bradley, North Carolina. They're either blissfully unaware of how many women are courting Miles, or they're overestimating his appetite. And the fact that Miles is an extremely picky eater." She brightened. "I suppose he's going to be receiving even more food now, considering Eloise's recent demise."

The talk of food made Myrtle hungry again, despite the generous breakfast Wanda had made earlier. So she and Wanda rummaged through the leftovers from Miles's lady friends and filled plates with a mix of different things.

They were just finishing up when the doorbell rang.

Myrtle frowned. "It's not quite time for Miles to come yet."

Wanda said with a sigh, "It's Dan."

"Dan as in Crazy Dan? Your brother?"

"The very one." Wanda took a last bite of her food and walked with Myrtle to the door.

It was indeed Crazy Dan, standing on Myrtle's front porch with his grizzled head, wild mangy beard, and a generous amount of stubble covering his leathery features. "Figured you was here," he said to his sister, completely ignoring Myrtle.

"Maybe you're psychic too," said Myrtle a bit snarkily. Dan seemed to always cause problems for Wanda to solve. He'd spend money they didn't really have, hoard things in their cramped living quarters, and generally loaf around.

Dan continued, "Needed some stuff in town and thought I'd see if you was ready for a ride back."

Wanda looked unconvinced so Dan continued, "Done some cleanin' up at the house, too. You should see it."

Now Wanda looked a bit more interested. Myrtle knew that ordinarily, if cleaning happened at the hubcap-covered hut, Wanda was the one behind it.

"Guess I could make it back now," said Wanda. She looked over at Myrtle. "That okay?"

"Of course, Wanda! Miles was going to step in, anyway. You can do whatever you need to do. Just keep in touch with me and let me know how things are going. You know that Miles and I will come pick you up anytime you'd like a break." The last was said with some emphasis, although Crazy Dan looked supremely unconcerned about whether anyone might need a break from his company.

Wanda turned right before she left. "Elaine's comin' in a couple of minutes. Needs you to babysit. She got to go to the doctor."

"Really? Okay, thanks, Wanda." She waved as Wanda and Dan climbed into a vehicle that looked like it shouldn't be allowed on the road at all. The car backfired and a cloud of black smoke spewed out the back before Dan started driving away.

Wanda was not only a good friend; she was also very handy to have around. Knowing that Elaine was coming over meant that Jack was also coming over. Myrtle pulled the cookie jar out, opened the small toy chest that held Jack's trucks and super-heroes, and waited happily until the doorbell rang.

Myrtle opened the door with a smile. "Elaine!" she sang out. But it was Miles there, looking confused.

"Oh, it's you," said Myrtle, looking rather deflated.

Miles frowned. "I thought I was supposed to come by here now and visit suspects with you."

"Don't be silly. We don't *visit* suspects, we *interview* them. And you are supposed to be here. Come on inside."

Myrtle whisked Miles in, led him into the kitchen and said, "We have a slight hiccup in our schedule today. Elaine is about to drop off Jack for me to babysit him."

Miles glanced around at the toys and the cookie jar and nodded as if it all made sense to him now. "I can come back later, then," he said, a hopeful tone to his voice.

"No, no. No need for that. We'll get Jack started playing and then we can recap what's going on with the murders. Wanda and I visited both Bailey and Marigold and it was all very interest-ing. I need to fill you in, since you're my sidekick."

The doorbell rang and Myrtle sailed back off to the front door. "Elaine!" she sang out again as she opened the door.

This time it was indeed Elaine, with Jack in tow. The little boy gave her a sticky grin—it looked like he'd gotten into some-thing sweet right before coming over.

Elaine had an apologetic look on her face. "Myrtle, I'm so sorry for barging in like this." She spotted Miles hovering in the background and said, "Hi, Miles! Wow, I'm messing up everyone's day."

Myrtle ushered them in and said portentously, "Let me guess. You need me to babysit, somewhat unexpectedly. You find that you need to go to the doctor."

Elaine gaped at her. "Myrtle! How did you know?"

"Easy. Wanda was just here and told me." Myrtle gave Elaine a thoughtful look. "But what's wrong?"

It was good that she asked because Miles was already pulling his hand sanitizer out of his pants pocket.

"Nothing catching," said Elaine hastily, sending an apologetic smile to Miles. "I think I have an ear infection. I figured I'd better get it checked out."

Myrtle crouched down and said to Jack, "Why don't you look for your toy box? I have a new toy in there for you. I forgot to give it to you last time."

Jack cheered happily and headed off for the kitchen.

"How are things going?" asked Elaine in a low voice. "I heard that you had something of an unexpected adventure last night."

Myrtle said, "I'm sure I probably woke you up with my phone call."

"That didn't matter at all . . . I'm used to Red being called away at all hours of the day and night. Are you doing all right, though? That must have been very upsetting."

Myrtle nodded. "Oh, I'm just fine. Poor Eloise, though." Myrtle's voice didn't sound very convincing.

Elaine, who knew Myrtle's opinion of Eloise, said, "Well, I'm sure it was startling, just the same." She glanced over into the kitchen where Jack was solemnly showing Miles his new dump truck and Miles was carefully looking it over. "I hear Red might have been asking both you and Miles some questions."

Myrtle sniffed. "It seems as though Red is convinced Miles or I have something to do with this. Maybe he thinks we were partners in crime."

Elaine shook her head. "He doesn't, Myrtle, I promise. He's just having to make sure everything is done by the book. You know how he is. He's mostly just concerned that you and Miles stay safe. Red's worried you're asking too many questions."

"Well, being considered a suspect can spur one to ask them," said Myrtle. "But thanks for saying that Red doesn't really think we've done anything."

Elaine glanced at her watch. "I'd better run. I don't think I'll be long—it should be a cut-and-dried appointment."

"Just be sure to go ahead and run by the pharmacy before you pick up Jack. There's no need to put him in a car and go back out later for your medicine," said Myrtle. "We'll be just fine."

Once Elaine left, Myrtle put cookies and milk out for Jack, Miles, and herself. Then they played Memory . . . a matching game that Miles and Jack both seemed quite good at. Myrtle's performance during the game was abysmal, but she felt the fact she was distracted by the murders was likely affecting her ability to find matches.

Miles said in an aside to Jack, "I don't think your Nana is very good at this game."

Jack chuckled and said, "Nana bad."

Myrtle said, "It's not that Nana is necessarily *bad* at the game, just that Nana is somewhat distracted."

Miles said, "I, for one, am delighted to find something you're not good at. I've lost far too many scrabble and chess games when playing you."

They played once more, Myrtle trying a bit harder this time to salvage her reputation as an excellent game player. But it ended much as it had before with Jack the decisive winner and Myrtle the decisive loser and Miles falling somewhere in-between.

Then Jack wanted to play with his trucks and some action figures he'd brought over with him. While he was busily making truck noises and giving life to the action figures, Myrtle filled Miles in on her morning.

Miles considered what she'd told him. "So Bailey did confess to both murders."

"Yes. But it doesn't count because he didn't kill anyone."

Miles said, "But he said he did."

"In a completely unconvincing way. He seemed very eager to turn himself in. And he'd given every appearance of being completely surprised when I said that Eloise died."

Miles looked reflective at the mention of Eloise. "I do feel badly about Eloise. The last time I saw her, I think I might have been rather rude."

"I was *always* rude to Eloise. That's because Eloise was a very difficult person. The fact that she's no longer with us doesn't make her an easier person. After all, you and I had absolutely no idea that Eloise was going to be murdered. And you needed to be firm with her since she wasn't getting the message that you two were no longer dating."

Miles sighed. "I know. Academically, I do know. But it's hard to escape the feelings of guilt that I have. And I've already been the recipient of more food this morning."

"As always, word travels fast. Just send as much food my way as you'd like. I'm still stretching my retirement check out a bit further. But going back to Bailey and Marigold."

"Bailey and Marigold?"

Myrtle said sternly, "Yes, our topic before you hijacked the conversation by waxing eloquent about Eloise. And I thought *I* was distracted today."

"Right. Yes, Bailey and Marigold. Bailey confessed, although he didn't seem to know exactly what he was confessing to. And you weren't impressed with his confession."

Myrtle said, "That's correct. Red wasn't either. Red said that Bailey didn't know important details that the killer would know. So Red didn't arrest him."

"So why do we think Bailey confessed?" asked Miles. "Did he just momentarily lose his mind? It seems unlikely, considering he ordinarily seems very sane."

"I think he was trying to protect Marigold. When I spoke with Bailey at Jax's service, he seemed very forgiving of Marigold's indiscretion and just wanted to make things right between the two of them. For whatever reason, I'm guessing he thought Marigold might be responsible."

Miles said, "That might have to do with the fact that Marigold and Eloise weren't really getting along."

"Mm. I gather there was friction between them since they were both seeing Jax. Perhaps that friction developed into something else."

"What did Marigold have to say?" asked Miles.

Myrtle sighed. "She's not very happy with Bailey. In fact, she's looking to end their marriage."

Miles raised his eyebrows. "She wasn't impressed by his gallant gesture? The fact that he was trying to shield her from being a suspect?"

"Not a whit. In fact, she seemed most annoyed with him for confessing. You see, by confessing, he basically admitted he was out of the house. So he messed up any alibi Marigold might have had."

Miles nodded. "Sounds like he didn't consider all the implications."

"Not only that, he didn't realize he didn't even have enough *information* to confess to two murders. It was all total nonsense. I could tell Bailey wasn't even aware Eloise had died when I told him about it."

The doorbell rang again and Myrtle scowled at it. "For heaven's sake. I wish I still had Wanda here to tell me who's out there."

"I know one way you can tell who's out there," said Miles pointedly.

Myrtle walked toward the door, her cane thumping on the floor as she went. She peered out the curtain then swiftly turned around and hissed, "It's Allen!"

Chapter Fourteen

Miles shrugged and Myrtle continued, "I'm not sure I should entertain a murder suspect with my grandson in the house."

Miles said, "Between the two of us, I think we can take him, Myrtle."

Just to be on the safe side, Myrtle gripped her cane very tightly, ready to swing it at the unsuspecting Allen at any moment. Then she opened the door.

Myrtle must have looked quite ferocious because Allen blinked in confusion at her. "Hi there, Myrtle," he said, stammering a bit.

"Hi," she said coolly.

Jack ran over to show them the new toy and Myrtle carefully took him by her free hand and kept him behind her. "That's wonderful, Jack," she said.

Miles stood up and walked over to help. "How about if I keep an eye on Jack in the back yard? That's the best place to play with trucks anyway. If you're all right with that?"

Myrtle gave him a relieved look. "Yes, that will be perfect. Come on in, Allen."

Allen walked in and sat down, glancing with interest at Myrtle's unfinished crossword. "I think five down is *ante*."

"Of course it is," said Myrtle crossly. "I've simply had a very busy day and haven't had the chance to fill it in."

"May I?" asked Allen. "I'm never able to get this far with crosswords, myself, and it's nice to look at an almost-finished puzzle."

Myrtle gave him a nod and Allen carefully wrote in the answer. "Do you always use a pen?"

"Most certainly. You have to have the courage of your convictions."

Allen gave a thoughtful nod. "Got it. Well, I'll try anything. Like I said, I haven't done too well with them."

Myrtle relaxed her grip on her cane a fraction. Still, she wanted to know exactly what sort of business brought Allen so unexpectedly to her house. After all, nothing was very welcoming in her yard right now. The gnome army was out in full force and carrying signs, for heaven's sake. And she'd never put out a welcome mat on the front porch. "Was there something I needed to help you with, Allen?"

Allen nodded. "I heard you had information about what happened last night."

"With Eloise."

Allen nodded again and looked a little embarrassed. "Sorry to bug you, but I wanted to find out what was going on. The cops keep asking me questions and I didn't even really *know* Eloise. I mean, I knew she was seeing Jax and that's about all I knew."

It was rather stunning that even Allen knew Eloise and Jax were dating and Miles and she were unaware of it. Either she and Miles didn't listen to much gossip, or else they simply weren't around it.

"Why do you think the police are asking you questions?" asked Myrtle. She gripped the cane again, remembering Marigold's assertions about Allen's vandalism of Jax's car.

Allen sighed. "You know . . . because of the animosity between Jax and me. Because he got me removed from the theater."

"Do you have an alibi for last night?" asked Myrtle.

Allen nodded eagerly. "I sure do. I told Red all about it when I saw him." He shrugged. "Like I said, I didn't even really know Eloise. I'm sorry she's dead, but I didn't have a thing in the world to do with it."

Myrtle nodded. She said briskly, "Excuse me for just a second, Allen, while I check on my grandson." She walked over to the kitchen window and looked out into her backyard. Miles had brought a notebook outside and had made a paper airplane, which was apparently fascinating to the little boy. Satisfied, she walked back over to Allen.

"Have a seat," she said, belatedly offering him a modicum of hospitality. Then she gave Allen a sizing-up type of look before saying, "I went outside to get some fresh air last night. Rather late. I was out on my dock and looking out on the water and I saw something floating in the lake."

Allen looked a little green. "And that something was Eloise?"

Myrtle nodded. "Red says it was murder. And it seems rather unlikely that Jax's murder and Eloise's wouldn't be connected . . . especially since the two of them were connected."

Allen swallowed.

"I feel as if Red needs a little help with this one," said Myrtle in a mulling voice. "I'm not saying my only child isn't competent, just that this perpetrator is sneaky. I'm trying to compile information for him . . . just to be of assistance, of course."

Allen looked a bit doubtful. "You're helping him solve these two murders?"

"Unofficially. Anyway, I'm trying to locate witnesses who might have seen something. Were you in this general vicinity last night? I'm not sure how long Eloise was in the water, which is somewhat limiting. Where were you last night?"

Miles came back in with Jack and Allen looked vastly relieved at the interruption.

"Jack seems to think his Nana might have some ice cream? Or popsicles?" asked Miles. There was a slight note of desperation in his voice.

"There are both. Not a lot of regular food, but plenty of frozen treats." She turned her laser focus back on Allen. "So . . . last night?"

Miles gave Jack a purple popsicle and watched with interest from the kitchen as Allen shifted uncomfortably.

"Well, last night I took your really excellent advice, Myrtle."

Myrtle quirked an eyebrow. "I always offer really excellent advice. Which bit, in particular, are you referring to?"

"Your advice that I approach Mr. Toucan about returning to the theater. You see, I think it was mainly my hurt pride. I couldn't take it that, after so many loyal years of service, Mr. Toucan could possibly think the worst of me and believe anything that Jax Jackson had to say. *Jax*! He wasn't the most reliable person in the world. You know that's true."

Myrtle nodded. "I'll grant you that."

Allen held out his hands. "I told him I'd never do anything to hurt the theater. That it was my 'happy place' all these years . . . where I'd go to de-stress. I told him I figured Jax just didn't like me or wanted me out of the way. Or maybe that Jax just felt like causing trouble of some kind between us—I'd say Jax had a mischievous streak."

Myrtle would have called it something more than merely mischievous. "What did Mr. Toucan say?"

Allen gave a crooked smile and said in a relieved voice, "He said I was welcome to come back. I got the feeling I'd be in a sort of probation period first, but I was so delighted to return to the Bradley Community Theater that I didn't really even care. I have you to thank for that, Myrtle."

"And that's what you were doing last night?"

"That's right." Allen's face grew somber again as he recalled that the reason they were talking about the theater at all was because he was establishing an alibi.

Jack came running in with purple popsicle all over his face.

"Goodness, Jack! Do you need your Nana to get that sticky off you? Let's find a warm washcloth for your face. That will feel good, won't it?"

"I should be going," said Allen hastily, as if fearing he was about to be drafted into childcare. He glanced over at the crossword on the table again. "Do you think the *flightless bird* might be *emu*?"

Myrtle bit back a retort. "Why don't you take that crossword with you, Allen? It looks like I'm having a busy day today and you might get more out of it."

Allen brightened. "Thanks, Myrtle. I stopped my newspaper subscription and I still really miss the crosswords."

He picked up the newspaper, waved while walking through the door, and disappeared.

Myrtle warmed up a soft washcloth and managed to get most of the purple off of Jack's face. She beamed at him. "You look just like your daddy did when he was a little guy, Jack."

Jack beamed back at her and stuck a finger in his mouth.

There was a light tap at the door and Elaine poked her head in. Jack trotted over and hugged her around the legs. "How did everything go?" she asked.

"How did everything go with *you*?" asked Myrtle. "We had a lovely time here, naturally."

Elaine said, "Well, I do have an ear infection . . . two, as a matter of fact. I have an antibiotic and am going to take a decongestant to try to clear my head." She sighed. "I think I'm going to have to miss my class, though."

Miles and Myrtle exchanged a look. Elaine was always trying new hobbies and they rarely went well. In fact, frequently, they were utter, outright disasters.

"What class is that, dear?" asked Myrtle with some trepidation.

"I'm taking a martial arts class. It's really wonderful from both a fitness standpoint and a self-protection approach. Of course, I don't suppose I actually need the self-protection part, considering I live with the police chief."

"Oh, I don't know—Bradley seems more treacherous every day," said Myrtle. "And you're enjoying the class?"

"Absolutely. I have a friend in there with me, too. Of course, I can't really go with an ear infection. I'm sure my head would end up throbbing like crazy. Maybe I'll be better soon, with the antibiotic." She reached down to ruffle Jack's hair. "Jack and I have had a time lately. Last night, he couldn't sleep because he was all keyed up and I couldn't sleep because of my ear hurting. So we went down to the community theater."

Myrtle raised her eyebrows and shared a look with Miles. "Did you, now?" Elaine had been a volunteer on and off at the theater when time allowed. Myrtle was just relieved that Elaine hadn't yet become part of the cast. She had a feeling that would not go well.

Elaine nodded. "There was a production last night of Agatha Christie's *The Mousetrap*. I wish I could have seen it. I let Jack run up and down the aisles and wear himself out and I helped Mr. Toucan pick up discarded programs."

Miles cleared his throat. "Did you happen to see Allen there at all?"

"Allen West?" Elaine looked surprised. "Was he supposed to be there?"

"He told us he was," said Myrtle in an ominous voice.

"Maybe he was at the theater at some point, but he wasn't there last night. Although Mr. Toucan said that he had talked to him a couple of days ago by phone and had reinstated Allen as a volunteer. I was glad he did because the theater is so important to him." Elaine looked concerned. "You're not saying that Allen's *alibi* is that he was at the theater? When Eloise died?"

"That's precisely what I'm saying. And it doesn't look very good for Allen, does it?"

Elaine shook her head. "No, it doesn't. But maybe he's just anxious about being considered a suspect. Maybe he had nothing at all to do with the murder and he doesn't have an alibi because he was at home in bed. He could have thought he needed to come up with something."

"It's very difficult to picture Allen as a coldblooded killer," said Miles.

Myrtle said, "That's because engineers have so little imagination, Miles."

Miles blinked as Myrtle correctly named his former profession for once.

Myrtle said to Elaine, "How are things going on Red's end of the case? What's his grumpy-meter set on?"

Elaine smiled. "He's pretty cranky, unfortunately. I believe the investigation isn't going as quickly or easily as he'd like."

Myrtle said innocently, "Red hasn't dropped any little tidbits, has he? Has he talked about any forensics information he might have gleaned from the state police?"

Elaine snorted. "As if Red would discuss forensic details with me."

"True. Or . . . has my wonderful Lieutenant Perkins been over for dinner with y'all? Have you been able to overhear the two of them talking about the case?"

Elaine said, "You get points for trying, Myrtle. But sadly, Lieutenant Perkins hasn't been around."

"He's probably too busy. Investigating two homicides will do that to you." Myrtle tilted her head to one side. "Perhaps you could send me a surreptitious text if Perkins comes unexpectedly to dinner."

Elaine chuckled. "Won't Red think it's very suspicious that I send a text and then you show up?"

"Not really. We could even set up a code."

Miles looked interested. "Codes can be fun. I used to create and send coded messages to my friends when I was a kid."

"Of course you did," said Myrtle, sounding not in the least surprised at Miles engaging in such a nerdy activity.

"What kind of code?" asked Elaine.

"Oh, I don't know. You mentioned picking up martial arts. You could say something like 'I achieved a purple belt today.'"

"There is no purple belt," said Elaine. "There is white, orange, blue, yellow, green, brown, and black."

"Even better for our purposes," said Myrtle complacently. "Then it really will be a special code. And that way I don't have to spend all of my time looking out my living room window to see if Perkins is across the street."

"*Have* you been doing that?" asked Miles, sounding doubtful.

"No. But I could have been."

Elaine said, "Okay, I think I can manage sending a code. And now, I should probably go. Jack's going to be needing a nap after all this excitement."

Myrtle said, "But he's been so good!"

"That's how I know he needs a nap. It's the calm before the storm." Elaine scooped him up and said, "Thanks so much to both of you for keeping an eye on him."

"Hope you feel better," said Miles.

Jack reached out and planted a sloppy kiss on Myrtle's cheek and she gave him a tight hug. "Darling boy."

After they left, Myrtle said, "I'm thinking if I crash the dinner with Perkins, I should bring something -with me to eat. Don't you think? I could just act as if I'd made it for myself and then bring it over."

Miles looked grim. "Although I liked the part about the codes, I'm less-certain about the rest of the plan. You don't even know that Red will host Perkins for supper."

Myrtle waved a hand breezily. "Oh, he always does. And he hasn't yet, or Elaine would have told me. I know—I'll make pudding for dessert. I haven't done that in ages."

Chapter Fifteen

M iles frowned. "Pudding. Isn't that complicated?"

"Pudding? Complicated? It's not brain surgery, Miles. It has only three or four ingredients."

"That sounds like the most dangerous type of recipe. The kind that appears simple but is actually very treacherous."

Myrtle ignored this. "I'll make it right now so I can be prepared at any time."

Miles shifted uncomfortably. "I thought we were going to continue your interviews. Isn't it time to speak with Nicole Jackson?"

"We'll speak to Nicole just as soon as I make this pudding."

Miles said slowly, "Do you even have all the ingredients?"

"Why are you being so contrary about my pudding? I'm certain that I have all of the ingredients." She hurried to the kitchen, cane stomping as she went. "As memory serves, I need cocoa, vanilla, and cornstarch. Or flour. Something."

Miles looked increasingly nervous. "Maybe it would be a good idea to locate the recipe. Do you remember what book it was in?"

"That might take the whole day," said Myrtle sternly. "Really, Miles. You have such a bee in your bonnet over this."

"I just think it would be much better to go off a recipe. Here, I'll look up pudding on the internet." Miles strode to Myrtle's small desk and started tapping at the keyboard. Myrtle sighed and peered over his shoulder.

"Here. This one looks easy." Miles's voice was relieved.

"They're *all* easy. That's the point of pudding."

Miles hit a button. "I'm printing this one out."

He carried the printout to the kitchen and pulled ingredients out of Myrtle's cabinets and fridge. "Sugar, salt, milk, butter, vanilla, cornstarch, cocoa." He frowned at the milk. "That's not enough milk, according to the recipe."

"Oh, it'll be fine," said Myrtle dismissively.

"It's not nearly four and a half cups."

"Then I'll simply add more butter," said Myrtle with a shrug.

"I don't think that's going to work."

Myrtle sighed. "You're getting all worked up over this. Why don't you go home for thirty minutes and then head back over? After that, I'll be completely ready to head over to see Nicole."

Miles looked as if he might have a lot more to say. But he clamped his lips together and quickly exited.

The problem, Myrtle decided at one point in the process of concocting the dessert, was that pudding had far too many dry ingredients. Everything seemed to explode everywhere when she took it from its container. At this point, she was going to have to have Puddin clean up the pudding. This amused her to think about and she laughed aloud, spilling a good deal more cornstarch in the process.

Once Tippy called her in the middle of the process to ask if she'd like to serve on a committee at church. Myrtle decidedly did not. After getting off the phone with Tippy, Myrtle reflected that it was certainly easier to say no to things when one was in one's eighties. After all, there were limited years left ... definitely too few to spend time doing things you didn't care to do. When she returned to the pudding, she wasn't at all sure where she'd left off with the recipe. She picked up with the cornstarch.

The conversation with Tippy had somehow taken longer than it should have. Tippy could be chatty. Looking at the clock, Myrtle turned up the heat on the stove to make up for the lost time. Then she set about trying to find her whisk. There was one particular drawer where the whisk should reside. She turned the drawer upside down on her kitchen table and went through every instrument ... no whisk. How did one lose a whisk?

She noticed a burning smell suddenly and turned the heat down to medium on the stove. Myrtle decided to use a fork instead. Sadly, the milk and sugar seemed to have scorched a little while she'd looked for the whisk, but she remembered there were many desserts that were revered for a smoky taste and were thought to be quite exotic. Smoked bread pudding was one of them, she recalled. So really, her smoked pudding would be *au courant*.

Myrtle poured the pudding into glass ramekins and put plastic wrap over them. Then she shoved them in the fridge. She checked her mail and smiled widely at an unexpected check from a medical overpayment. Then she looked at the clock. She was just thinking that Miles should be coming over at any time when there was a tap on the door.

"Hi there," she said, opening the door wide to let him in.

Miles walked in cautiously. He sniffed the air and made a face. "Did something happen with the pudding?"

"Yes. The pudding was cooked."

Miles said, "No, I mean beyond being cooked. In fact, it smells as if it might have been cooked a little too much."

"As a matter of fact, the pudding was smoked. It's a very modern approach to pudding," explained Myrtle.

Miles frowned at this. He walked into the kitchen and paused. "Wow."

"What?"

Miles said slowly, "The mess."

"Oh yes, I know. Everything exploded everywhere when it was being measured. Pudding has too many dry ingredients." Myrtle put her hands on her hips, still troubled over the missing equipment. "You haven't seen my whisk anywhere, have you?"

"Did you *have* a whisk? I'm not sure I've ever seen you whisking anything."

"Of course I have a whisk! Everyone has a whisk. It's practically a rule for homeowners. What would I do if I wanted to whisk egg whites?"

Miles knit his brows. "I've never known that whisking egg whites was something you aspired to."

Myrtle bored of the subject. "Let's go see Nicole. First, though, I'm going to see if I can get in touch with Puddin."

Miles gazed around the kitchen again. "Puddin might balk at this."

"I can handle a balking Puddin. Anyway, she balks at every-thing: dust, crumbs on countertops, dull furniture. It's nothing new."

Puddin did indeed balk on the phone. Her voice was sus-picious on the other end of the line. "You say there's kitchen mess?"

"Yes. There are some dry ingredients on the counters and floors. Maybe on the kitchen table, too."

Puddin said, "My back is thrown, Miz Myrtle."

"Your back is always thrown at the most inconvenient of times, Puddin. But here's the real problem—if the kitchen stays like this then I'm going to be tracking the dry ingredients all over the rest of my house. The problem is going to worsen expo-nentially."

Miles agreed with this and could be heard in the back-ground saying, "I'll be tracking it around, too."

"So you see, Puddin, we must take immediate action."

There was a distinct groan on the other end. Then Puddin said in a crabby voice, "Guess I'll come over then."

It was hardly gracious, but about right for Puddin. Myrtle said, "Good. You know where the key is, don't you? Miles and I will be out conducting some business."

"Under that gnome, ain't it?" muttered Puddin.

"You'll have to be more specific than that. There are quite a few of them out there right now, courtesy of Dusty."

Puddin growled, "Put it under the one with the fishin' pole, then."

"The darling one with the red fishing pole and the impish expression on his face? Why Puddin, I didn't realize you had a favorite in my collection."

There were more, rather dire, mutterings on the other end and Myrtle cheerfully said, "See you soon, then."

"Are you? Going to see her soon?" asked Miles.

"It remains to be seen, as it always does with Puddin. I'll get more done if I disable the television somehow. Sometimes I accidentally disable it anyway by pressing the wrong button on the remote."

Miles said, "Do you remember how you disable it? It sounds like a very effective way to keep Puddin from watching game shows when you're not here."

Myrtle walked over to her remote and pointed it at the TV. "I think it's this 'input' button here. I'm always trying to hit the 'mute' button and hit this one by accident."

Miles studied the remote. "I can imagine that hitting input would shut things down."

"Especially if I hit input and then select a service that I don't pay for. One of those streaming ones. I have the feeling that Puddin wouldn't be able to find her way out of that. She doesn't strike me as the kind of person who's very tech savvy."

"No. No, she doesn't."

Myrtle sighed. "The only problem is that *I* might not be able to find my way out of the input labyrinth. Once I had to call Red. That was most annoying."

Miles pushed his glasses up his nose. "I think I should be able to help you out with the remote. You shouldn't have to call Red over it, at any rate."

Myrtle beamed at him. "Perfect. The less I can rely on my son, the better."

She hit a few buttons on the remote and watched as the screens on the television became ever more puzzling and incomprehensible.

"Perhaps that would be a good place to stop," said Miles, looking slightly nervous. "If you keep pressing buttons, I may not be able to follow the breadcrumbs out of the forest. Besides, I'm pretty sure Puddin will be stumped by what you've got up on the screen."

Myrtle nodded with satisfaction. "And with nothing else to do, Puddin will have to address the disaster in the kitchen. Now, let's head over to see Nicole."

Miles shifted uncomfortably. "I certainly hope we're not having to go to the salon. I can't think of a plausible excuse for my being there."

"That you're my driver, of course. I don't have a vehicle of my own, as you well know."

Miles said, "Why don't you call the salon and figure out when Nicole is working. That way we're not driving all over town looking for her in various places."

Myrtle did call them. And, as it happened, Nicole was due at the salon in the next thirty minutes.

"Pooh," said Myrtle. "Now we'll have to wait. If we go over to her house, it won't give us enough time before she has to go to work."

Miles said, "Why don't we take a walk? I could stretch my legs a little."

"Fine. As long as we don't linger too long in front of Erma's house. I don't think I have it in me to deal with an Erma encounter."

Miles cautiously stuck his head outside the door, looking both ways. "The coast is clear."

They hastily passed Erma's house then breathed a sigh of relief. There was a brisk breeze blowing, which made the walking very tolerable. Myrtle thumped her cane emphatically as she walked down the sidewalk. Dogs barked at them from nearly every house.

Miles gave a startled exclamation and Myrtle followed his gaze. "Pasha!" she said. "What a clever girl. Are you following us on our walk?"

"If she's so clever, why did she brush up against *my* legs?" muttered Miles. "She just about gave me a heart attack."

"You shouldn't be so jumpy, Miles. Pasha was merely saying hello. Oh look—there's Sherry, out in her yard. Wanda mentioned her last time and I've meant to visit and see if she can provide a clue to this investigation somehow. Goodness, but she does a lot of yard work. She always makes the rest of us look awful in comparison."

Sure enough, Sherry was cheerfully deadheading roses with her pruners. She stopped when she saw them and came over to chat.

"How's it all going?" she asked. "Myrtle, I haven't seen you at the gym lately."

Myrtle said, "I know. I've been taking my exercise in other ways lately."

Sherry raised her eyebrows. "Why do I have the feeling you've been tackling our latest crimes in Bradley? I saw your article in the paper recently."

Myrtle did her best to appear modest, failing utterly. "Well, you know how it is. Always something happening here in town. It only *looks* like a quiet place."

Sherry nodded. "There's always all sorts of drama happening here, that's for sure." The word *drama* apparently called something to mind and she looked over at Miles. "How are you holding up, Miles?"

Miles looked unhappy at being associated with drama. "Oh, I'm doing fine. Keeping busy."

Sherry said, "I know it's wicked to speak ill of the dead, but I can't help it. I think Eloise treated you just abominably. You're well rid of her."

Miles appeared to badly want to change the subject. "What types of neighborhood drama are you alluding to, Sherry? Anything interesting going on?"

This time Sherry tactfully refrained from mentioning Eloise, her cheating, and her untimely death. "Well, let's see. There's a feud going on between Hampton Ridgeway and Lois Kerby. Hampton was spotted putting her dog poop bags into Lois's trash bin."

Myrtle snorted. "That was dumb on Hampton's part. Everyone knows Lois spends the day looking out her front window with binoculars." She gave a cheery wave in the direction of Lois's house, figuring she was being watched.

"Exactly," said Sherry.

Miles didn't look particularly impressed by this bit of drama, so Sherry dug deeper into her memory. "Prentiss Mabrey said that Robert only leaves his house to mow the grass and go to the liquor store."

Myrtle raised her eyebrows. "I've noticed he mows his lawn just about every single day. I do hope he's not imbibing at the same time he's operating the mower."

"Hm," said Miles, still looking rather unfazed by all the neighborhood gossip.

Sherry brightened as something occurred to her. "Speaking of drinking, your editor actually is a lot more fun than he looks."

Myrtle knit her brows. "Sloan is?"

"Surprising, isn't it? I was out with Nicole Jackson last night and we ran into him."

Myrtle said slowly, "You're friends with Nicole?" There was quite an age difference between them. Sherry could be Nicole's mother.

"Sure! Well, I was friends with her mom and then sort of adopted Nicole as one of my own kids after her mom passed away. Nicole also does a great manicure, if you haven't been." Sherry waggled her multi-colored nails at them.

"Actually, I've been to see Nicole at the salon." Myrtle showed off her own nails and Sherry looked impressed by Myrtle's daring.

"Anyway," continued Sherry, "I took Nicole out with me last night to cheer her up a little. It's been real hard on her, you know, with Jax's death and everything. I thought she could do with a night out. We ran into Sloan there, sitting at the bar."

"Unsurprising," murmured Myrtle.

"We got to talking with him and before you knew it, we were all singing a song along with the jukebox." Sherry grinned in remembrance.

"I wish I'd been able to see that," said Myrtle. She would actually have liked to have taken a picture and posted it on the *Bradley Bugle's* social media accounts.

Miles said slowly, "So Nicole was out last night, then."

"She certainly was. We had a great time," said Sherry firmly.

Myrtle said, "What time did all of your shenanigans—the singing and whatnot—end?"

Sherry shrugged. "Oh, I'd say it was around nine-thirty. I started getting sleepy with all the beer. I'm not young like Nicole was, so I headed on home. But I was glad that I had the chance to cheer her up. She's missing her dad, of course. On top of that, though, she's also worried about money."

Myrtle recalled that the topic of money seemed to come up fairly frequently in conversation with Nicole. "She wants to move from Bradley, I believe? She mentioned moving to Atlanta."

"Well, that's what she *wants* to do, but the problem is that she just doesn't have the money. And she was really appalled at how long probate takes. It's really a full year or thereabouts. She won't be getting any of that estate money for a while."

Myrtle nodded. "It certainly does take some time." She glanced at Miles. "We should let you get back to your beautiful yard, Sherry. Miles and I are going to take a walk and then we thought we'd go over to the nail salon and get manicures."

Sherry beamed at Miles, who reddened. "That's a wonderful idea. And Miles, kudos to you! Most men are so silly about manicures. I'm glad to hear you're man enough to get your nails done. I have seen some men who are in *dire* need of a manicure or pedicure, let me tell you."

As Myrtle and Miles walked away, Miles muttered, "I thought we'd agreed that I was going to be your driver, only."

Myrtle said brightly, "I realized how good it would be for your reputation among the merry widows of Bradley if you got a manicure. You were always pegged as the sensitive sort because of your book club picks, but this will really cement your legacy."

Miles sighed. "I'm pretty sure I don't need any more attention from the merry widows than I'm already getting."

"Just the same, get the manicure. It's clearly not as rare as you think because the salon has it up on their 'services' menu."

Miles said, "Your nails don't look like they need another manicure. Are you just wanting to get a different color?"

"I'm getting a pedicure this time," said Myrtle complacently. "That will give me plenty of time to speak with Nicole. And they take a bit of time so it's good that you're getting a manicure so you won't be waiting too long."

Miles gave her a sideways glance and said delicately, "I thought pedicures were fairly expensive things to get."

Myrtle said, "Yes, they are. But guess what I got in the mail yesterday? An unexpected refund from my doctor's office for overpayment. Isn't that wonderful? That *never* happens."

"And it's burning a hole in your pocket?" Miles asked dryly.

"It certainly is. I'm unaccustomed to such riches. So I'll spend a bit of it on the pedicure today."

They walked around the block so they wouldn't have to pass Erma's house again and risk an encounter. Then Miles drove Myrtle over to the salon.

Chapter Sixteen

Miles walked into the nail salon with some trepidation, but was relieved to see that it was a very businesslike, clean décor. "I thought it might look like the Beauty Box salon where you get your hair done," he murmured.

"It's not nearly as fussy or prissy," agreed Myrtle.

Nicole came over to greet them, wearing a sparkly red top and black capris. "Good to see you two! What can I do for you?"

"I thought I'd get a pedicure today. I suppose I should match the color with my manicure or I might look quite wild. And I was able to talk Miles into a men's manicure, if there's someone available who can help him with that."

"Absolutely," said Nicole briskly. "Follow me."

Myrtle grabbed the bottle of nail polish and retreated into the back of the salon as Miles sat down with a woman who immediately started soaking his hands.

Nicole put a liner into the pedicure tub and carefully adjusted the temperature of the water for Myrtle. Then she started chatting with her, which was just what Myrtle wanted.

"I heard about Eloise. It's getting very creepy in town with a killer unleashed like this. Has Red made any progress?"

Myrtle snorted. "If he has, he hasn't shared that information with me. I'm hoping to be able to attain some information from Lieutenant Perkins from the state police shortly. I've made a special pudding to bring to dinner when Red hosts him."

"Are puddings hard to make?" Nicole expertly pulled out her clippers, files, and other tools.

"Goodness, no. But they do make a terrible mess."

Nicole said, "So you think you might be able to find out how the cases are going from Perkins? I'd like to hear if there has been any progress on my dad's death. I haven't heard anything from law enforcement except for questions."

"Perkins is a bit more forthcoming sometimes. We'll see. After all, I'm an investigative reporter and I need to write my next piece on the case for Sloan soon." Myrtle paused and then said, "Speaking of Sloan, I heard from Sherry that you and she hung out with him some last night. And that singing was involved."

Nicole chuckled. "It was quite the evening. I have the feeling Sloan probably woke up with a headache this morning. He was really drowning his sorrows last night."

"Well, he has quite the convoluted love life. I think he drowns his sorrows on a semi-regular basis." Myrtle paused and then said, "I'm sure, working here, that you probably hear a lot of local gossip."

Nicole grinned at her. "Do I get to be a source for one of your articles? If I am, I don't think my clients will open up to me anymore. And that might be a blessing or a curse—I'm not sure which."

Myrtle said, "Oh, not for an article. I can't print rumors, of course. But I'd love to hear what the local gossips are saying, in general."

Nicole said, "They're saying that Bailey Pratt has lost his mind."

"Really?"

"I guess *not* really, but he's certainly very distracted. Some have said that he confessed to my dad's murder."

Myrtle pressed her lips together. She really didn't want to confirm that information. "Is that so?"

"And that's not the only thing. He clipped somebody's car in the parking lot. It was bad enough to get his insurance company involved."

"Mercy."

Nicole continued, "And one of my ladies told me that she was behind him in the line at the Piggly Wiggly and he walked out without paying for his groceries. The poor check-out girl had to chase after him. He was apparently very embarrassed."

"I'm sure anyone would be. I wonder what he must have on his mind to do such a thing."

Nicole said sharply, "On his mind . . . or on his conscience? If he's responsible for my dad's death, I want him to face justice. I know people are saying that his confession didn't add up, but maybe he did that on purpose to deflect attention from the fact that he really *is* the murderer."

"You're saying he acted as if he didn't have any of the real facts about the murder when asked so that his 'confession' made it look as if he were actually innocent," said Myrtle.

"Exactly. I'm not saying Bailey did it, but he's sure acting really odd. Or guilty. He's not the kind of person who ordinarily behaves like that, you know? He's always been this really organized guy who manages a very successful career from everything I've always heard."

It certainly was interesting. Considering that Bailey's original alibi for Jax's murder had been that he'd carefully been charging his devices after a business trip, it seemed like he wasn't the sort of person to be behaving in a very absentminded fashion. He clearly did have something on his mind, but what was it?

The pedicure progressed very nicely and Nicole chatted about all sorts of other Bradley-related gossip. It appeared that there were many people in town with quite a few skeletons in their closets.

When she was done, Myrtle admired the matching color on her toes. Nicole put her in a pair of disposable flip-flops and took her over to a dryer to get her polish dried. Miles was already done with his manicure and seemed pleasantly surprised as he surveyed his hands.

"They do look better. Healthier," he said thoughtfully.

"That's what I was saying. It's a nice service, isn't it?"

Miles said, "Your toenails look good, too. Nice matching color. But you're not going to be walking around in those foam flip-flops, are you?" He cast a look at the orthopedic shoes she'd come in with which looked a lot sturdier and more appropriate for an octogenarian to walk around in.

"No, I'm going to sit under the dryer until they're totally dry. No worries."

It took some time. Enough time that Miles started reading an old copy of *Vogue*. But then they were able to pay and take their leave. Nicole gave them a cheery wave as they left.

"Back to your house?" asked Miles as he started up the car.

"Oh, I think so. Otherwise, Puddin might be goofing off and doing no cleaning whatsoever."

"Even without a functioning TV?" asked Miles.

"Certainly. She might be dozing on the sofa. It's always important to keep her on track."

Sure enough, as soon as they walked into Myrtle's house, they were confronted with the sight of Puddin holding a remote and looking completely confounded. She'd apparently been completely focused on the task at hand and jumped when they walked in the house.

Puddin leveled a furious look at Myrtle. "TV's broke."

Myrtle said, "I'm fully-aware of that. What's the status of my kitchen?"

Miles peered over into the kitchen and winced.

"Never mind," said Myrtle. "Apparently, it's the same disaster area it was when I left."

Puddin muttered, "Shoulda told me the TV was broke."

"Absolutely not. There's no reason for me to disclose any issues with any of my entertainment gadgets with the person who's here to clean up my house."

Puddin narrowed her eyes at Myrtle. "Maybe I like to play the TV in the background when I work."

"The problem is, when the television is on in the background, you tend to drift back to it. The television acts like some sort of homing device."

Puddin sighed. She walked over to the kitchen, squaring her shoulders. She called behind her in a catty voice, "What happened in here, anyway?"

Myrtle said offhandedly, "The dry ingredients exploded."

Puddin turned to glance directly at Miles. A look passed between them that Myrtle couldn't quite define. "Better get to it," said Puddin, slouching into the room.

"And don't use my cleaning supplies!"

Miles and Myrtle settled into the living room, Miles on the sofa and Myrtle in her armchair. Miles said, "Did you get any good information from Nicole? It sounds like she *could* have murdered Eloise, from what Sherry was saying. She was out last night, at any rate."

Myrtle could tell that Puddin had paused in her cleaning. She supposed Miles and she were now functioning in the place of the television. "Pay no attention to us, Puddin."

There were some grumblings from the kitchen as the sound of very lackadaisical cleaning started up again.

Myrtle said, "What I mostly gleaned from our conversation, was that Bailey Pratt seems to be under quite a bit of duress."

"That was already apparent, though, wasn't it? He confessed to a crime that he seemed not to have committed. It's not the most rational thing to have done."

The cleaning sounds from the kitchen stopped again.

"Puddin!" hollered Myrtle, making Miles jump.

Puddin's pale face peered sourly around the corner of the kitchen door. "I got a right to hear stuff like that, Miz Myrtle."

"But it doesn't have anything to do with you. You're just looking for gossip that you can share with your cousin, Bitsy."

Puddin's features darkened. "That Bitsy always has better gossip." She wandered fully into the living room.

"Well, you're not going to one-up Bitsy with anything that we're talking about. We're having a private conversation. A private conversation that Miles and I are now going to conduct in the backyard." Myrtle stood up.

Puddin tilted her head to one side. "I might have some gossip, too."

"I'm assuming any gossip you have comes from Bitsy," said Myrtle.

This insinuation irritated Puddin. "I hear stuff, too!" she said furiously.

Miles cleared his throat. "What exactly did you hear?"

Puddin gave Myrtle a triumphant look at being asked the question. Then she lowered her voice to make her gossip sound more ominous. "That guy from the theater? You know him?"

"You mean Allen, I suppose?" said Myrtle stiffly.

"Yeah, that's him. Bitsy says—I mean, *I* heard—that he slashed a hole in that dead man's tire."

Myrtle pursed her lips. "Yes, I'd heard the same thing. But it was just conjecture on Jax's part. He didn't actually know the identity of the person who'd committed the vandalism."

Puddin screwed her face up as she tried to digest what Myrtle had said. "Keep tellin' you to speak English."

Miles helpfully interpreted. "Jax, the dead man, was just guessing that Allen had slashed his tires. He didn't actually know that."

Puddin suddenly looked smug, realizing she knew something they didn't. "But Bitsy cleans across the street from Jax. She saw Allen do it."

Myrtle and Miles exchanged a glance. "And Bitsy's sure of that?" asked Myrtle.

Puddin gave her a scornful look. "Course she is. Saw him right as she was comin' out of the house to get in her car. He had a box cutter out and was slashin' at the tires somethin' fierce."

"I guess he was unhappy with Jax," said Myrtle mildly.

Puddin said, "Mad enough to kill him, maybe."

"All right. Now enough of all that. I need you to go ahead and finish up in that disaster of a kitchen. Otherwise, I'll end up having somebody like Tippy Chambers drop by, for sure, just to embarrass me."

While Puddin reluctantly addressed the kitchen, Myrtle and Miles moved outdoors to talk. They walked gingerly down to the lake and sat on Myrtle's dock to watch the water.

"So, you said Bailey Pratt was falling apart," said Miles, trying to remember what the thread of conversation had been before Puddin had totally hijacked it.

"Nicole did. She hears things at the salon like Bitsy and Puddin hear things when they're cleaning. Anyway, he has apparently been very absentminded. Nicole said he clipped a car in a parking lot. And he walked out of the Piggly Wiggly without paying for his groceries."

Miles frowned. "And this was *Bailey*?"

"Yes. That's the surprising thing. He always seemed to have his life together. What do you supposed caused it all?"

Miles thought about this for a few moments as a sailboat went by on the lake. "I suppose it could have to do with Marigold. From what I understand, he's completely devoted to her."

"And Marigold doesn't seem half as devoted back," said Myrtle. "In fact, I think Marigold has another paramour. Maybe Bailey is so focused on how to win Marigold back that he's distracted in every other way."

"Confessing to murder seems like rather a stretch, though," observed Miles.

"Yes. But Nicole wondered if his confession was a cover of some sort."

"A cover?" asked Miles.

"That's right. She thought Bailey might have killed Jax and Eloise and then given a ridiculous confession to distract the police from the fact he actually killed them. That Bailey was making it look like he *hadn't* killed them when he had."

Miles said, "That seems like a very convoluted plan and one that could easily backfire. Besides, I thought we'd just established that Bailey was so distracted that he was making all sorts of mistakes. It seems strange that he would have chosen that particular approach to deflect attention from himself."

Myrtle shrugged. "It wasn't my theory, it was Nicole's."

Miles looked at his watch. "What's next? You've spoken with everyone, haven't you?"

"I have. So now we should watch *Tomorrow's Promise*. Then I'll wait for Elaine to provide her code word for us to come over and try to get some information from Perkins."

Miles raised his hands as if warding off an attack. "Oh, no. I'm not part of your Great Supper Caper. I'm staying put at home tonight and eating a tomato sandwich with cheese."

"What? I thought you and I were going to drop in over there together."

"Nope," said Miles soundly. "You and your pudding and your gate-crashing activities are all you."

"Well, pooh," said Myrtle.

"What are you trying to find out from Perkins, anyway? It sounds as if we might be further ahead than the police as it is?"

Myrtle said, "How do you figure that?"

"We have the information from Puddin, courtesy of Bitsy, that Allen was responsible for Jax's slashed tires. That sounds like something the police don't know about."

Myrtle shrugged. "The way Bitsy talks, it's entirely possible that the whole town, including the police, know all about it. Anyway, I want to find out more about Eloise's death. And I feel as if I have the responsibility to make sure that neither you nor I are considered as suspects. I'd like the time of her death, for instance. Maybe you and I were otherwise occupied during that time."

Miles said, "I hardly think Pasha is a good alibi for you. And I was completely alone."

Myrtle gave him a stern look. "You really need to stop saying that. It makes you sound very guilty."

"I find myself *feeling* guilty, even though I had nothing to do with Eloise's death. It seems as though I should have been protecting her."

Myrtle quirked an eyebrow. "Being her knight in shining armor? How gallant of you, Miles. However, the uncomfortable truth remains the same—Eloise's death was the fault of Eloise. You had nothing to do with it and had no responsibility for her since the two of you weren't a couple any longer."

"I suppose that's true," said Miles, perking up a little.

"I always speak the truth," said Myrtle airily. "You know that."

Miles said, "If we're just in waiting mode now, I might as well go home and take a nap. I'm feeling pretty worn out from the last week."

"All right. I'll let you know if I get a signal from Elaine. It's about the right time in the investigation for Red to want to hash things out with Perkins, so I'm keeping my fingers crossed that it's tonight."

After Miles went home, Myrtle went into her house, made sure Puddin was still working on the kitchen disaster, and then proceeded to "fix" her television.

Puddin called out from the kitchen, "Hey! How'd you do that?"

Myrtle sniffed. "I have all sorts of talents, Puddin. Fixing TVs just happens to be one of them."

Puddin narrowed her eyes suspiciously as if fairly certain Myrtle's skills with electronics weren't usually something to write home about.

Myrtle watched a little television but didn't find anything to keep her interest. She decided to go through her copy of *The Importance of Being Earnest* and mark it up for her book club talk next time. She reminded herself to keep the discussion on a more simplistic level, considering the apparent limitations of the group.

At some point, Myrtle dozed off. When she awoke, the kitchen was clean and the money she'd left on the table for Puddin was gone.

She'd just decided to watch her tape of *Tomorrow's Promise* when she got a text message.

I'm getting purple belt tonight at six-thirty it read. It was, of course, from Elaine.

Myrtle smiled to herself. Then she frowned at the clock. Six-thirty was only fifteen minutes away. She definitely wanted to change clothes for dinner with Perkins so she put on a pair of black slacks and a dressy top. Then she took the puddings out of the refrigerator. Myrtle pulled the saran wrap back on one of the ramekins to peer at it. It was fairly chunky looking to Myrtle's eye. Perhaps, she decided, it was because it was especially thick. But no one would want *runny* pudding. Thick was good. Satisfied, she covered the pudding back up and then packed up a tote bag and proceeded across the street.

Red opened the door, a wry expression on his face. "Just happened to be dropping by, Mama?"

"I had a culinary triumph and decided to share it with my family," said Myrtle, putting her nose in the air and sailing past him into the house.

Elaine, looking slightly flushed, called out to her from the kitchen. "Myrtle! What a lovely surprise!"

Chapter Seventeen

"**I**sn't it?" said Myrtle. She put down her tote bag and gave Jack a huge hug. He ran off to bring her a toy to show her. Lieutenant Perkins rose from the sofa to greet her and she gave him a hug. "So nice to see you again, Perkins!"

Red was still looking at the tote bag with distrust. "What's this culinary triumph you were talking about?"

"Pudding. It's absolutely delicious."

"Is it? Have you tasted it, Mama? Because it seems to me that not sampling your own recipes is one of your failings."

Perkins seemed to be concealing a smile.

Myrtle said breezily, "I didn't have to taste it. I just gave it a visual inspection. It looked just fine and will be a perfect dessert for our dinner."

Red glowered at her. "You're not planning on staying for dinner?"

"Well, of course I am! Goodness, Red, you're acting as if you and I never enjoy a meal together."

Red gave Perkins an apologetic look.

"I'm delighted at the opportunity to visit with you, Mrs. Clover," Perkins said promptly.

Myrtle beamed at him. "We'll have a wonderful time, won't we?"

Red said, "The problem, Mama, is that you're here with an agenda."

"An *agenda*? What a silly thing to say, Red. My agenda is simply to have a nice visit, see my darling grandson, and distribute puddings."

"I think the agenda has more to do with the signs your gnomes are holding. I was hoping that the rainstorm the other night would have destroyed them, but no such luck," said Red.

Myrtle said smugly, "That's because I carefully put them in gallon-sized zipper bags."

"Very ingenious," said Perkins.

Myrtle smiled at him. "I thought so. And since we're already on the topic—"

"Here it comes," said Red with a sigh.

"I wondered if Miles is no longer considered a suspect. I suppose I should also ask about myself, since I believe I might have been under suspicion, too."

"Mama, no one seriously thinks an octogenarian is drowning people in the lake," said Red, rolling his eyes.

"Well, that's certainly very shortsighted of them."

Red said, "So now you're trying to talk yourself into being a suspect?"

"I'm just saying that I *could* have done it. I didn't, but I could have. I had no motive to kill Jax, of course, but that Eloise drove me up a wall. Besides, she was most unfair to Miles."

"That's the part that makes *Miles* a suspect," pointed out Red.

"As if Miles could harm anybody or anything. If you look up the word 'innocuous' in the dictionary, it probably has a photo of Miles by the entry."

Red muttered, "It sure won't have a photo of the puddings you brought."

Perkins seemed to be trying to cover up that smile again. Then he quickly said, "I don't think anyone seriously considers Mr. Bradford a suspect, Mrs. Clover."

Myrtle folded her hands in her lap and looked satisfied. "That's good to hear. I might have another question or two."

Red put his head in his hands.

"Stop being so dramatic, Red. Curiosity is a good thing. It's supposed to slow cognitive decline. Anyway, I was wondering about Eloise's untimely death. Have you narrowed down the time it happened?"

Red glanced over at Perkins as if asking how much they wanted to disclose. Perkins said carefully, "We think it might not have been very late in the evening. The water does obscure the time of death a little. But it probably wasn't too much later after the victim had her encounter with Mr. Bradford."

Myrtle sniffed. "It wasn't much of an encounter, really. It was Eloise trying to be pushy and Miles firmly telling her things were over. That woman was really in a state of denial."

Perkins said, "It does sound as if she was."

"She thought she could have her cake and eat it, too. Having a relationship with two men at once . . . absurd!"

Perkins nodded. "I was hoping I could ask you a question in return, Mrs. Clover."

But just then, Elaine called them to supper. Jack had already been apprehended by his mother and placed in a booster seat at the table. He grinned at Myrtle, showing off his baby teeth. He appeared to be eating something gelatinous and colorful that Myrtle fervently hoped would not be served to the adults at the table.

Fortunately, Elaine put a lasagna on the table just moments later, relieving Myrtle's mind tremendously. She helped her plate and put some garlic bread on the side.

"It's lucky Elaine made enough food for all of us," muttered Red. Then he looked thoughtfully at his wife and mother.

Myrtle decided a distraction was in order before Red realized Elaine was in league with her. "Perkins, you mentioned you had a question for me."

Perkins carefully put some lasagna on his plate. "You always do an amazing job investigating."

Myrtle straightened in her chair, looking pleased. Red continued muttering, this time under his breath.

"I was wondering if you've uncovered anything interesting pertaining to the case," continued Perkins smoothly.

Myrtle paused, her desire to show off warring with her instinct to keep her findings under wraps. She did so like to solve a case before her son did. She pasted a regretful look on her face and said, "I'm afraid everyone has not been forthcoming. They're all very stingy with the information they give out. I'm coming up with nothing."

Now Red was looking pleased. And Perkins was considering her thoughtfully. "That's interesting," Perkins said slowly. "And unusual, too. I know ordinarily people spill all kinds of gossip to you."

"True." Myrtle picked up her glass of sweet tea. "Folks in town do like to talk. But I suppose this time they're wanting to just keep their thoughts to themselves for one reason or another."

Fortunately for Myrtle, Jack decided to be charmingly distracting right then. He was blowing raspberries and grinning at them. The raspberry sounds were making the disgusting-looking substance he was eating spray everywhere and Red hurried off to get a paper towel to clean him up.

The conversation turned to other topics then. Myrtle asked after Perkins's mother, who was also a puzzle aficionado. "She's taken up bridge, too," said Perkins. "Do you play?"

"Not any longer," said Myrtle.

Elaine chortled. "Myrtle beat everyone at bridge and no one wanted to play with her anymore."

Perkins chuckled and Red added, "This has actually been a recurring theme throughout Mama's long retirement. No one will play scrabble or canasta with her, either. She may even have been banned from chess."

"I'm not good at chess." Myrtle waved her hand dismissively.

"You may not think you are, but how many invitations have you gotten to play it lately? Even Miles won't play games with you anymore."

"We do puzzles together," said Myrtle with a shrug.

"Sometimes it's best to stick with non-competitive activities," said Elaine.

Myrtle was doubtful of this philosophy but didn't argue the point. She glanced around at everyone's plates. "It sure looks like it's time for pudding."

Red was shaking his head before she'd even finished the sentence. "Can't. I'm stuffed. I ate far too much pasta and garlic bread."

Elaine quickly added, "I'd better put Jack down. Sorry, Myrtle. I'll be sure to have some after lunch tomorrow. You were awfully sweet to bring it."

Perkins cleared his throat. "I'd be pleased to have some, Mrs. Clover."

Myrtle beamed again at him. "Excellent! I'll have some, too. I always have enough room for pudding." She said this with a sideways glance at Red who hastily got up and collected the dinner plates to put in the dishwasher.

Myrtle collected the puddings and put one in front of Perkins and one at her own place setting. "Bon appétit!"

Myrtle took a big bite of her pudding and Perkins took a somewhat more conservative bite as Red watched, smirking, from the kitchen.

Myrtle knit her brows as she swallowed down the pudding. "Hm. It's quite chewy for a pudding, isn't it? I think that's what I like most about it. It's not like those watery puddings out there."

"It's nice and thick," said Perkins after he'd taken a large sip of water. "Chunky, as a matter of fact."

"Yes, I think so, too."

Perkins quickly finished his pudding like a man on a mission as Myrtle watched in amazement.

"Goodness, but you were hungry! Would you like some more?"

Red called out from the kitchen, "You can have mine, Perkins!"

Perkins said carefully, "That's very generous of you, Red, but I can't take your portion. Besides, it was very filling and I'm completely full now."

Myrtle took another mouthful and swallowed it down with some difficulty. "Yes, it is, isn't it? Very filling. I might be finished with mine, myself."

Red took the pudding containers to wash out as Elaine came back into the room. "Well, Jack's in his bed, although I'm not sure he'll stay there."

"Would you like some pudding?" asked Myrtle.

Elaine patted her tummy. "I'm still really stuffed, Myrtle, but thanks. I'll save the treat for tomorrow. Would you like to say goodnight to Jack? He's still awake in there, for sure."

"That would be perfect. Then I'll take my leave and let all of you continue with your evening."

Red looked relieved. "Need me to escort you back home, Mama?"

"Certainly not! It's directly across the street."

"Yes, but it's getting dark out there," said Red.

Myrtle glared at him. "I know how to cross the street by myself. I don't need an overgrown boy scout helping me. Besides, I have a cane." She lifted it up threateningly at Red, who quickly backed off. Elaine and Perkins shared a smile with each other.

Myrtle walked back to Jack's room where her grandson was definitely not sleeping but was instead looking at a book by the light of his nightlight. He was wearing dinosaur pajamas and grinned when he saw Myrtle.

"I have a hard time falling asleep sometimes, too," said Myrtle, giving Jack a hug. "Want me to read the story to you?"

As it happened, the picture book was all about dinosaurs. Apparently, there had been more types of dinosaurs discovered since Myrtle had been reading dinosaur books to Red. She stumbled over most of the names, which seemed to have far too many consonants in them. Jack carefully corrected her with no judgment at all. By the time she'd finished the story, Jack was looking sleepy.

Myrtle tucked him in and walked back out into the living room. Red and Perkins had been talking but quickly became quiet when she entered the room. "Jack seems to be falling asleep now," she told Elaine.

"Well, you must have worked some real magic on him. I was sure he was going to be up for a while," she said.

"I think he became exhausted while correcting my pronunciation of dinosaur names. I never realized there were so many," said Myrtle.

Red said, "Apparently the scientific community has been working very hard discovering new dinosaurs and naming them. I'm not sure why they couldn't stick with easy names. Some of Jack's dinosaur books are total tongue-twisters."

They chatted for a couple of moments about dinosaurs, Red apparently trying to get back into his mother's good graces after irritating her over the pudding and the offer to escort her home. Then Myrtle thanked Elaine for supper and took her leave.

Instead of walking back home, Myrtle headed toward Miles's house. She spotted some quick movement from the bushes and was joined by Pasha.

"Clever girl! Were you keeping an eye out for me? I'd rather have you escort me than Red any day. Would you like to go visit Miles?"

Pasha smiled up at her, green eyes shining.

Miles looked less than delighted when he opened his door.

"Pasha and I have come to say hi," said Myrtle.

Miles opened his door wide and Pasha strode in, making a swift lap around the house to ensure she accurately remembered where all the entrances and exits were. Then she settled down next to Myrtle on the sofa.

"How did everything go at Red's?" asked Miles, a wary note in his voice.

"Oh, it was fine. Although it wasn't *extremely* helpful. I did get an approximate time of death for Eloise, although we had something of an idea for that. Apparently, she died not too long after speaking with you."

Miles sighed. "I had the feeling that was the case."

"I did press them over whether you and I were suspects. Red acknowledged quite snarkily that I wasn't much of a suspect." Myrtle scowled, still feeling a sense of injustice over this.

"I suppose there aren't very many octogenarian murderers."

"Red is very limited in terms of his imagination. Anyway, there was a bit more hesitation over whether you're still considered a suspect but Perkins acknowledged that you weren't very high on his list of possibilities."

Miles looked relieved. "That's good. I wasn't looking forward to the idea of spending my golden years in prison."

Myrtle nodded. "You'd have a hard time fitting in. There probably isn't much Faulkner in the prison libraries." She paused. "They also tried pumping *me* for information, but I resisted. I told them that I hadn't been able to find out anything—that people had been remarkably close-mouthed."

"And they believed that? That people in Bradley hadn't been gossiping?"

Myrtle shrugged. "They appeared to accept it. I'm a good actress."

Miles asked, "And what happened with the dessert?" He had a watchful look on his face.

"Elaine had baked a lasagna and garlic bread and Red and Elaine had so many carbs they were too stuffed to try the pudding."

Miles nodded in a knowing way. "And Perkins?"

Myrtle said, "Perkins *loved* the pudding. As did I. The only problem was that the dessert was so thick and chunky that it was quite filling, too. But he and I ate most of ours."

Miles said carefully, "The pudding was . . . chunky?"

"Yes, it was. Which was a vast improvement over the thin, watery puddings I so often see."

Miles nodded. "Right. Well, moving forward, what are we doing next? Investigation-wise, I mean."

"At this point, we're going to need to try to ferret out more information. Maybe we can go out and about a bit more and see if we can run into some of our suspects around town. Now that I have my medical refund, I can afford a trip to Bo's Diner."

Miles sighed again. "The problem is that I don't feel much like being out and about right now."

Myrtle frowned at him. "What? You're not feeling well?"

"It's not that. It's just that I have the terrible sensation that everyone is looking at me when I go out."

"That certainly sounds like paranoia, Miles. Perhaps we should get you to your doctor."

Miles shook his head. "It's not paranoia when it's true. You know what it's like in Bradley. People talk. When I'm out running errands, people are either looking at me like I murdered Jax in a homicidal rage because he was seeing the woman I was dating, or else they're looking at me with pity because Eloise cheated on me and is now dead."

Myrtle said sternly, "Miles, if you're going to continue living in a small town, you have to adopt the attitude that it doesn't matter what people think."

"It's easier for you to say that. People don't talk about you."

Myrtle snorted. "People don't talk about me? Are you out of your mind? That's the main reason Red wants to hide me away in Greener Pastures Retirement Home. People have talked about me for decades. I'll remind you that I have sign-holding gnomes in my front yard."

"Well, that's true." But Miles still looked glum.

Myrtle tilted her head to one side thoughtfully and stroked Pasha. "You need some cheering up. I know. Was there anything from your childhood that made you cheer up? Something that you found comforting?"

Miles thought about this. "The Howdy Doody show."

Myrtle said dryly, "I meant something that's still attainable. Besides, if you watched the Howdy Doody show now, I doubt it would have the same effect. What about comfort foods?"

Miles knit his brows together. "You're not proposing cooking it, are you?" In fact, meatloaf had come to his mind immediately, but he certainly didn't want to task Myrtle with that. He quickly added, "Beanie Weenies."

Myrtle blinked at him. "You surprise me, Miles. You seem far too refined for franks and beans. Won't it play havoc with your delicate digestive system?"

"I haven't had it for decades," said Miles slowly. "But I can't imagine a small bowl of it would do much harm."

Myrtle stood up and headed in a decisive manner toward the door. "I'm on it, Miles."

"You don't need to go *now*. It's dark outside. And I've already had supper." He saw the determined set of Myrtle's chin and quickly added, "Myrtle, I'll go with you."

"Don't start sounding like Red. It's very tiresome. A walk will do me good after all the pasta, bread, and pudding I consumed tonight. It's all starting to sit like a brick in my belly. Anyway, I'll be just fine and don't require you to accompany me. Pasha will be with me."

Pasha, watching from the sofa, looked interested in this theory. Being a feral cat and belonging to no one, she felt under no contractual obligation to accompany Myrtle. But the night was her favorite time and she loped after Myrtle when she opened the door.

Because Myrtle was on a mission, she strode briskly to the grocery store, cane thumping in time as she went. Pasha trotted quickly to keep up and the cat didn't allow herself to become distracted by night sounds along the way.

The grocery store, after the dark walk over, was almost garishly bright. Myrtle let herself get adjusted to the light and then headed off to the soup aisle where she suspected she might find the franks and beans. Pasha stayed outside the store and promptly proceeded to give herself a vigorous bath.

Myrtle decided if a can of Beanie Weenies were helpful, several would be even better. That way, Miles could dispense them whenever he was feeling blue. She cradled the cans in one arm while leaning on her cane with the other.

After she'd paid for the groceries and the young bagger had bagged them, Myrtle headed back out into the night again. Pasha watched her a short way away as if trying to decide whether she wanted to stay out in the night or wanted more time with her human friend.

Myrtle absolved her of any responsibility, "You can go hunt things if you want to, Pasha. I'm just fine."

Pasha blinked at this, as if not altogether sure. Then she slipped farther into the darkness as a voice called behind Myrtle. "Miss Myrtle?"

Chapter Eighteen

M yrtle turned. "Oh, hi Nicole."

"Is everything all right? That bag looks heavy."

Myrtle nodded. "The bagger double-bagged it though, so it won't break."

"I was more worried about you being able to carry it home," said Nicole. "It doesn't look like you have a car here or that anybody dropped you off."

"That's very sweet of you, my dear. But I'm really just fine. How are things with you?"

Nicole shrugged. "I guess things are moving along. Probate is taking forever. One of my clients mentioned that I should just go to the bank and take out a small personal loan and go ahead and move to Atlanta."

"I see. So then, when probate goes through, you can pay off the loan. It does make sense. Are you going to be sorry to leave the salon? Or, actually, this type of business altogether? I know you mentioned you'd be pursuing fashion."

Nicole said, "Of course there are parts that I'll miss. I'll miss my clients most of all. But I've always had a flair for the dramatic that I just can't satisfy with manicures and pedicures. I used to do a lot of acting when I was a kid—there were summer camps and drama clubs at school."

Something struck a chord in Myrtle, but she couldn't quite put her finger on it. "So you spent time in the theater," she said slowly.

Nicole gave her a funny look. "That's right. Have you heard anything from Red about the case? And—speaking of the theater—has he been asking Allen about the car tires?"

"Oh, Red won't tell me a blessed thing about the case," said Myrtle vaguely. Then she thought about a flair for the dramatic. Her soap opera. And tea. She leveled a serious look at Nicole. "So you can be pretty dramatic, is that right?"

Nicole's funny look grew a bit more strained. "Sure. I mean, not all the time, but I can be."

"Does it happen when your emotions get all riled up?" asked Myrtle conversationally.

Nicole gave a short laugh. "I guess so."

"Like when you lose your temper. Over something, perhaps, like a potential windfall from a real estate deal that your dad refused to cash out on."

Nicole's eyes narrowed. "What are you saying, Miss Myrtle?"

"Just that flinging tea at someone seems to fit in with the personality of a person who has a flair for the dramatic." Myrtle gave her a serious look.

Pasha growled from a dark place nearby.

"Tea?" Nicole was now apparently trying to backtrack and act as though she didn't know what Myrtle was talking about.

"I know all about the tea, Nicole, as you clearly do, too. Eloise, bless her, spilled that bit of information to us before Red cautioned her not to mention it to anyone. You may not know this, but Wanda is my friend."

Nicole didn't say anything. Pasha came out of her dark hiding spot and stood near Myrtle, still making that rumbling growl to express her displeasure at what was unfolding.

"Wanda is a psychic," continued Myrtle. "And she mentioned tea. And, actually, drama. Plus, there was my soap opera."

Nicole said in a low voice, "Miss Myrtle, you're not making a lot of sense."

"Yes, but isn't that precisely what happens when everything starts tying together? All these little bits and pieces of information and images and suddenly all the pieces of the puzzle start falling into place. It's a truly amazing process. But the sad fact of the matter remains—you killed your father." Myrtle tilted her head to one side. "I wonder, though, if it might not have been intentional. Was it an accident? You were clearly very wound up at the time. Jax was a stubborn man and he wanted to stay in his house on his land. You're a young person with no ties who wanted to start a new life somewhere else."

Pasha was staring ferociously at Nicole with her fur puffed up.

Myrtle said, "You were frustrated and you do have, as you put it, that flair for the dramatic. You threw your father's hot tea at him. He must have screamed, stumbled around. Did he hit his head? Fall? Is that what happened?"

Nicole made a growling sound of her own and lunged at Myrtle. Myrtle reared back and swung the bag of Beanie Weenies at her as hard as she could.

It was apparently quite hard because Nicole went down on the sidewalk. Pasha started caterwauling—a shrill wailing.

Which is right when the young bagger came fearfully out of the store, cell phone in hand.

"Help!" called Myrtle. "I've been mugged!"

Despite, of course, all evidence to the contrary. The alleged mugger was out cold.

The bagger did call the police and an ambulance for good measure. Red was there in what felt like seconds. When he arrived, Myrtle was sitting demurely on a bench nearby, the bag of canned beans and franks next to her as she held her cane in a threatening way over the prone figure on the ground. Pasha, having ensured Myrtle was all right, bounded off into the night to do some hunting.

"Assault, Mama?" asked Red in an exhausted voice.

"Thanks for asking," said Myrtle crisply. "Yes, *she* was about to assault *me*. Fortunately, I still possess very quick reflexes and was able to beat her to the punch."

The ambulance pulled up and Myrtle and Red watched as EMTs started working on Nicole.

"What exactly happened?" asked Red as more police cars arrived. "The bagger said there was a lot of racket outside and then she saw 'an old lady clobber a young woman with her groceries.'"

"A poor description of the events, but at least she called for help when prompted." Myrtle gave a sniff. "I was speaking with

Nicole after shopping. She'd approached me, allegedly to help me with my heavy bag."

"Allegedly." Red looked toward the heavens.

"As we were speaking, all sorts of things came to mind. Nicole described herself as dramatic. I started thinking about the tea. And Wanda. And *Tomorrow's Promise*, too."

Red rubbed his forehead and then his left eye as if there was a throbbing he couldn't quite reach.

"Throwing tea at someone is a rather dramatic gesture, isn't it? It's not just something one does every day. Nicole was very upset with her father and that was how she decided to show her displeasure."

Red said, "Not by killing him?"

"I never really got to the bottom of that, but here's what I suspect: Jax's death was an accident. Nicole threw hot tea at his face and he staggered about his kitchen before falling and hitting his head. She never meant for it to happen, although she certainly stood to benefit from it."

Red said slowly, "So you came to this conclusion and then walloped Nicole with your groceries."

"Don't be silly. I confronted Nicole with my conclusions and realized she knew all about the tea. And *no one* knew about the tea except for Eloise, Miles, me, and the police. And, of course, the killer. She charged at me and *then* I walloped her with my cans of Beanie Weenies. Pasha started howling and the young bagger came to see what was going on."

Red nodded wordlessly.

"Sadly, she didn't regain consciousness. I'd have liked to inquire over Eloise's death, but I didn't get the chance."

They watched as the EMTs were able to revive Nicole. She looked woozy and confused but then her gaze sharpened and she started glancing around her. Myrtle gave her a cheery wave and Nicole briefly closed her eyes again. It looked, to Myrtle, like an admission of defeat.

"Did you kill Eloise, dear?" called Myrtle, still focused on solving the last piece of the puzzle.

"I did *not*," said Nicole defiantly.

Red hastily intervened, "We're going to talk all about that at the police station."

Nicole refused to go to the hospital for more care, so the EMTs got back into their ambulance and left. The state police, headed by Lieutenant Perkins, were already hustling Nicole into a car.

Then Perkins joined Red and Myrtle. "Are you all right, Mrs. Clover?" he asked with concern.

"Fine and dandy," said Myrtle with a chipper smile.

Red said to Perkins, "I'm going to take Mama back to her house and then I'll be right over at the station."

Myrtle said, "I really don't need an escort, as I told you earlier tonight."

"I'd say this episode proved that you *do* need an escort. At least in order to prevent other people from being attacked with your groceries."

Myrtle sat primly in the passenger seat of Red's police car as he headed back to her house. After a moment she said, "If Nicole didn't murder Eloise, then I wonder who did."

Red groaned. "Mama, you need to leave this to the professionals. You've already done enough tonight."

"Yes, I have. I have single-handedly found and disabled Jax's killer," said Myrtle smugly. "That's quite enough for one night, I think." She could hardly wait to tell Miles.

"So you're going to turn in now and go to sleep, aren't you?" There was a note of suspicion in Red's voice as if he thought Myrtle's nocturnal activities might not be done for the day.

"For heaven's sake, Red. It's ten o'clock. I'm not a child."

"I was just thinking that it might be good for you to put your feet up and take it easy. You've had a big evening. I mean, *I'm* tired and I'm in my forties."

"Barely," Myrtle helpfully pointed out.

"And I had a lot of carbs for dinner that are making me feel like I could drop off to sleep at any moment."

"Octogenarians keep different hours," said Myrtle.

"Oh, I'm aware of that."

"Besides, I have to write my article for the *Bradley Bugle*. It won't run in tomorrow's paper, of course, but Sloan may even want to release a special edition. Or an online 'breaking news' piece."

Red muttered under his breath.

"After that, maybe I'll be able to fall asleep."

Red drove rapidly away after he walked his mother to her door. Myrtle got right on the phone and called Miles.

Despite the early hour, Miles sounded suspiciously like he might have been sleeping.

"Guess what!" said Myrtle triumphantly.

Miles hazarded a guess in a drowsy voice. "The pudding upset your stomach."

"Don't be silly, Miles! It did no such thing. I solved the case and Nicole is arrested!"

There was a pause. "I'm coming over."

"All right, but I'll have to kick you out rather precipitously. I have an article to write for Sloan."

Miles appeared a few minutes later wearing hastily adorned khaki pants and a button-down shirt that seemed to be incorrectly buttoned-up. He was also a good deal more alert than he had been.

"What happened?"

Myrtle filled him in as Miles listened, frowning. From time to time he interjected a question.

At the end of her recital, he said slowly, "It was accidental then."

"That's what I'm assuming. I suppose it might count as manslaughter, but I really don't know. At any rate, she's in trouble. She didn't report a death and she tried to assault me."

Miles knit his brows. "That must have been scary."

"Well, I sort of saw it coming, so it took away the element of surprise. After all, I was pushing her. Once it all came together, though, I really couldn't help myself."

"And she *didn't* have anything to do with Eloise's death?"

"That's what she said."

Miles said, "And we're sure that a murderer's word is good?"

"We're not, actually. But I'm open to the possibility that someone else murdered Eloise."

"That means there are two murderers in Bradley." Miles looked distinctly dissatisfied by this idea.

Myrtle shrugged. "It's happened before. The important thing is to stop them before they can kill again. We've already taken care of Nicole. And now we need to shut down Marigold."

"Marigold!"

"Don't sound so shocked, Miles. Marigold is the natural choice for a second murderer."

Miles said, "I don't see how you're coming to that conclusion. We just heard that Allen slashed Jax's tires. It seems as if he's a more-likely candidate."

"The problem with Allen is that he had a better motive for killing Jax. But *Nicole* killed Jax. The only reason Allen could have for wanting to murder Eloise is if she knew he was responsible for Jax's death. Which he wasn't."

Miles closed his eyes. "You're making my head hurt."

"Look at it this way—even Bailey thought Marigold was the killer. That's why he came up with that crazy confession of his . . . he thought he was protecting his wife."

Miles said, "And Bailey really *couldn't* have done it?"

"It sure doesn't seem so. He didn't know things that the killer should have known. Besides, Marigold had a good reason for wanting to kill Eloise."

"Which was?" asked Miles.

Myrtle sighed. "You really should be paying better attention. Marigold doesn't have an alibi. And Eloise was spreading lies about Marigold—and they were definitely lies. She was telling everyone that Marigold had killed Jax. Marigold would have wanted to shut Eloise up for good."

"What are you going to do now?" asked Miles with some trepidation.

"I know exactly what I'm going to do. I'm going to write the story for the paper. But tomorrow morning I'm going straight to Perkins and ask him to put me in a sting operation."

Miles just blinked at Myrtle disbelievingly.

"A sting operation is just a method the police use to act deceptively to catch someone who they believe to have committed a crime."

Miles said, "Yes, I'm familiar with sting operations. I just don't completely follow how you and the police would ensnare Marigold."

"I'd bait her, of course. And I'd be wearing a wire and record everything that came out of her mouth."

Miles frowned. "Are you sure that the Bradley police department has wires and taping equipment? That seems sort of high-tech. We're talking about a police station that has vinyl furniture and two cells."

"Of course they don't have that sort of equipment. But Perkins would. The state police are probably rife with it. After I get Marigold's confession, I can write an amazing story about the experience for the newspaper. I bet it's another article of mine to be picked up on the news wire and run in other papers." Myrtle looked very pleased with herself.

"It all sounds rather unsafe. Baiting suspected murderers and such." He shifted uncomfortably in his chair and then bravely said, "If Perkins agrees to it, I'll go with you. Just to make sure everything goes smoothly."

Myrtle didn't actually like this idea at all. There was a limit to how much glory a sidekick should get. This covert operation was entirely her plan and she wanted to do it solo. "We'll see.

For now, I'm going to write this piece for Sloan for the paper or the paper's blog. We'll have a big day tomorrow, so be sure to get some sleep."

"I don't think I'll sleep a wink," said Miles grimly.

Chapter Nineteen

Miles apparently didn't, because when she arrived at Miles's house bright and early the next morning, he looked bleary-eyed at her and was still wearing plaid pajamas and a navy bathrobe and slippers.

"What's happening?" he asked, looking a bit confused.

"We're going to the police station, remember? I need to tell Perkins about our plan."

Miles stumbled back into his house and Myrtle followed him. He sat down in an armchair. "Myrtle, this is *your* plan. I'm not altogether sure it's a good one. Plus, won't it qualify as police entrapment or something? I'm positive Lieutenant Perkins won't want to be party to some sort of entrapment scheme."

"No, no. Police entrapment is when officers push someone who *hasn't* committed a crime into committing one. Sort of a 'gotcha' thing. This is completely different. This is a person who murdered someone but hasn't confessed."

"Allegedly," said Miles. "A person who *allegedly* committed a crime."

Myrtle frowned. "You're being quite gallant over Marigold's involvement, Miles."

"I'm just trying to view her as innocent until proven guilty," said Miles a bit priggishly. Then he added, "I'm going to need to drink some coffee if we're going to engage in philosophical conversations about the justice system. Would you like some?"

Myrtle shook her head absently. "I've already had several cups. Did you not get any sleep last night?"

"Very little. And then, when I did sleep, I dreamed about Marigold getting the third degree in a windowless cell."

"You're quite obsessed with this, you know. Besides, all I'm going to do is have a friendly conversation with Marigold. Taped. And I do think it will be far more effective if I approach her alone."

Miles made the coffee, which looked very strong to Myrtle's eyes. Quaffing a cup of it quickly, he disappeared to get ready for the day.

Myrtle fretted a little while he was gone. "Do you think Perkins will be at the police station? Or might he be out in the field somewhere?"

Miles muttered something from the back that Myrtle couldn't hear.

"Perhaps I should give him a call instead. That way I'd be sure to get him."

This time Miles's voice was louder. "You have his phone number?"

"Of course I do. Perkins and I are friends. He told me to call him anytime. And I believe that's just what I'm going to do."

Miles came back into the living room now sporting his omnipresent khakis and button-down shirt. "Isn't it very early to be calling anyone?"

Myrtle looked at her watch. "It's seven a.m. I've been up for four hours already and I'm sure Perkins has already started his day." She took out her phone and started pressing buttons.

Fortunately, Perkins was indeed awake and sounded very alert. "Mrs. Clover. What can I help you with this morning?"

"Good morning! I have an idea I'd like to share with you."

Myrtle set about explaining her scheme while Perkins listened quietly on the other end of the line.

When she wrapped up, Perkins said slowly, "That's a very interesting plan, Mrs. Clover. But it also sounds as if it could be a dangerous one. Tell you what—I'm about to head to the police station now and meet up with Red. How about if you come over and cover what you've just told me again in person. I feel an obligation to loop Red in on this idea."

"Must we? Red is such a party pooper."

Perkins sounded as if he might be suppressing a chuckle. "I can't really see a way around it."

"All right, then. See you in about fifteen minutes." Myrtle hung up the phone and sighed.

Miles arched his eyebrows. "So Red is getting involved?"

"Unfortunately so. Apparently, Perkins has some sort of personal ethics standard or something."

"Well, he *is* a police officer," said Miles.

"I suppose so. Are you ready to go?"

They hopped into Miles's car for the short drive downtown to the police station. When they walked into the building, Red was standing there looking worried. The red hair that provided his nickname was standing straight up on his head as if he'd been running his hands through it. Perkins gave them a welcoming smile.

"Mama, what's this nutty plan you have?"

"Good morning to you, too, Red! Are you having a good day so far?" asked Myrtle cheerfully.

"Not really," grumbled Red. "Fill me in, please."

So Myrtle did. Red looked more agitated as she explained it all. Miles took a seat on the vinyl sofa and tried to make himself seem very small and inconsequential as Red's inner turmoil increased.

"What do you think?" asked Perkins a bit cautiously.

"I think my mother has had a small stroke," said Red.

Perkins said, "The problem I see is the inherent danger of the set-up."

Red snorted. "Oh, I think my mother can take on Marigold. We're talking about the woman who felled Nicole Jackson, fifty years her junior, with cans of franks and beans."

Myrtle straightened. "Well, I have to say I'm pleasantly surprised to hear this enlightened view from you, Red. It's about time."

"That doesn't mean that I think it's a good idea for you to badger Marigold into confessing. For one thing, we're not altogether sure she's to blame for Eloise's death," Red told her. Then to Perkins he said, "Mama doesn't *know* anything. She bases her clues on psychics and soap operas."

Myrtle said, "That's the beauty of this approach, though. We can find out for certain."

Perkins was quiet for a few moments and then said, "We have currently hit something of a stumbling block, Red. And I'll admit that Mrs. Clover has a gift for making people open up to her."

"They underestimate me," said Myrtle with satisfaction. "To their everlasting detriment."

Red rubbed his temples. "So we're talking about putting a wire on my mother and sending her over to speak to a murder suspect."

Myrtle put her hands on her hips. "Do you have any better ideas right now? Nicole says she didn't murder Eloise. Ergo, there's another killer still on the loose in Bradley. That means it could be only a matter of time before this murderer strikes again to cover up the crime."

Red and Perkins looked at each other. Finally, Red sighed and said, "Okay. If you and Perkins want to give this a go, I won't stand in your way. Although I do think it might end up being a tremendous waste of time and resources. How are you planning on getting Marigold on her own?"

Miles cleared his throat and they all looked a little startled, having nearly forgotten he was there. "I do know that Bailey is planning to be at chess club at lunch today. At least, during our last meeting he said he was planning to attend. I believe he likes the Cuban sandwiches we have there."

"Excellent," said Myrtle. "I'll go see Marigold at home in just a few hours, then."

Perkins said, "Are we planning on having Mr. Bradford accompany Mrs. Clover for backup?"

Miles was about to bravely offer to escort Myrtle when she quickly said, "Oh, I don't think so. It will look much more like some sort of intervention if Miles and I both confront

Marigold. No, I think she'll be much more likely to feel comfortable enough to confess if he's not there. Just wire me up and I'll be the solo agent."

Red rolled his eyes.

Hours later, Myrtle was carefully wired up. She insisted on walking over to Marigold and Bailey's house so that no one would see her being dropped off in a police car. She was a bit out of breath when she finally arrived. Perkins and Red were parked inconspicuously on the road behind the house.

Myrtle strode right up to the Pratts' house and knocked on their door. The door opened and Bailey stood there.

Myrtle gave him an annoyed look. He wasn't supposed to be there. She tried to cover up her annoyance and said sweetly, "Goodness. I thought you'd be at chess club with Miles. I know Miles told me that was today."

Bailey said, "Well, I was planning on going, but then I realized I had to enter all of my expense reports before the end of the week. Figured I'd just get caught up with my paperwork since I'd already put it off for a while." He paused. "Sorry, did you have business with Marigold?"

"Is she around?" asked Myrtle. She could already hear Perkins in her ear saying that she should abort the mission. She decided to ignore the voice.

"She's not, but she should be in after a while. Maybe you'd like to come back." Bailey was already shutting the door and backing away.

"May I wait for her?" asked Myrtle, still in that sweet voice. "I just wanted to have a little chat with her. I know she's involved with Chancel Guild at the church and I figured I'd ask her about it."

Myrtle was rather proud of her wild improvisation. She had no idea if Marigold was involved whatsoever with Chancel Guild, but considering how often Bailey traveled, she figured he wouldn't know either.

Bailey frowned, but let Myrtle walk inside. "Chancel Guild? Marigold's not in Chancel Guild."

"Isn't she? Perhaps I'm remembering her involvement from long ago."

"She's not particularly involved in church whatsoever." Bailey's frown grew a little deeper. "You wouldn't be prevaricating, would you?"

"I'm simply interested in volunteering my time."

Bailey snorted. "You're simply interested in being nosy."

Myrtle peered at him with interest. "You think she did it, don't you?"

Bailey stared wordlessly at her.

"You think Marigold killed Jax in a jealous rage."

"You're delusional," he said coldly.

"Not at all. I'm putting it all together," said Myrtle. She tilted her head to one side in a considering manner. "You must not have been out of your house yet today."

"I've been working on paperwork, as I've already mentioned." Bailey's tone was brusque.

"So you wouldn't have heard the news. Nicole Jackson was the one responsible for Jax's death. It seems to have been an unintended consequence."

Bailey grew very still.

"The problem was," Myrtle continued blithely, "that you believed Marigold killed Jax. This has caused you to behave in all sorts of illogical ways. You even made a quick confession in an effort to cover for your wife."

Bailey muttered something and Myrtle got closer to him, worried that her microphone wouldn't pick up what he was saying. "What's that, Bailey? You have to speak louder than that when you have octogenarian guests in your house."

"I was saying," bellowed Bailey, "that the police said my confession was worthless because I didn't know all the details concerning the crime."

"That was certainly true for Jax's murder. You wouldn't have known how Jax died because you weren't there. You believed Marigold had killed him. Then, when Eloise started blabbing around town that Marigold had been responsible for Jax's death, you decided to eliminate her. Your confession for Eloise's death was fabricated to sound just as clueless. The difference was that you knew the details of Eloise's death perfectly well since you were the one who killed her. It's funny—when I told you about Eloise's murder, you seemed surprised at the time. I thought that was because you hadn't heard the news. But actually, you were just surprised she was so quickly discovered. You must have thought you'd have more time."

Bailey's forehead had beads of sweat on it and he stepped back a couple of paces from Myrtle.

"That makes you feel a little sick, doesn't it? You believed Eloise knew something about Marigold's involvement with Jax's death. But there was no need to kill Eloise. She was just a gossip in a town full of them. Eloise posed no threat to Marigold whatsoever. You killed her for no reason at all—Marigold is completely innocent."

Bailey continued perspiring. His skin had a decidedly green tint about it.

Myrtle said, "It's rather amazing that you were so determined to see your wife as guilty. I can't help but think it had to do with the fact that she didn't have an alibi for Jax's death. In fact, I wonder if she could have been out that night."

Bailey said gruffly, "So she was out. It doesn't really matter now, does it? You just said that Jax's daughter killed him."

"Marigold has given every impression that she's moved on from your relationship. I think she may even have been tiring of her fling with Jax. She may have someone completely new she's seeing now. And I believe *that's* what you didn't want to face. You'd rather believe that she was murdering Jax than having another affair."

Now Bailey's eyes held a desperate shine to them.

"Did you hit Eloise on the head with something first? Or just shove her in the water?" asked Myrtle like a teacher quizzing a student.

"Miss Myrtle," said Bailey with a short laugh, "No one even knows for sure if Eloise was murdered at all. She couldn't swim. Seems to me she might just have fallen into the water."

Myrtle regarded him solemnly. "That's very interesting that you know she didn't swim. That was something Eloise was embarrassed about and didn't speak of."

Bailey turned red and then white. He said in a dangerous voice, "Miss Myrtle, I can't believe that you were silly enough to approach me about this. I'm really sorry, but I can't let you tell your son what you've found out."

"So you admit it," said Myrtle quickly.

"It was an accident. I didn't realize she couldn't swim. I was just furious with her—threatening her with a lawsuit for defamation. She was telling everybody in town that Marigold had killed Jax and I thought she had a *reason* for saying that."

Myrtle snorted. "Eloise didn't have a reason for saying anything."

"She fell in and called to me. She said she couldn't swim." Bailey's eyes were unfocused as if he were right back in the moment.

"And you didn't rescue her."

Bailey held his hands out in a pleading gesture. "I froze up! There was nothing to hand to her, either. No buoys or life vests or anything. If I'd jumped in to help her, she probably would have drowned me, too." He took a step closer to Myrtle. "That was an accident," he repeated. "And I hate that you're making me do this on purpose. You're an old lady. The oldest in town."

Myrtle said sharply, "No. That honor goes to Irabelle at Greener Pastures."

Bailey had just grabbed hold of the fireplace poker when Perkins, Red, and a couple of other police officers barreled into the house with their guns drawn.

Bailey's jaw dropped.

Myrtle said, "Beware of old ladies, Bailey."

Minutes later, Bailey had been read his rights and was in a police car with a couple of state policemen questioning him.

Marigold had returned and was watching from a distance with a scowl on her face.

Myrtle, Red, and Perkins were in the front yard of the Pratt home.

Red said in a somewhat snarky tone, "I thought we were trying to arrest Marigold. That seemed to be the whole point."

Myrtle shrugged. "It became clear to me that Bailey was the perpetrator, not Marigold. You heard it all unfold. Besides, he shouldn't have known that Eloise couldn't swim. That was something only those very close to her knew."

"Well, I guess all's well that ends well. And you didn't even have to clobber anyone with groceries this time."

Perkins gave Myrtle a concerned look. "Are you okay? That must have been a really stressful thing to go through, even though it did turn out just fine."

Myrtle decided to play it for all it was worth. "Maybe lunch at the diner would be good. It might make me a little steadier on my feet." She wove a bit worryingly and Perkins took her by the arm.

Red said, "Mama's just looking for a free lunch, Perkins. Her retirement check doesn't come in for another day or two."

Myrtle leveled a blistering glare at him.

Perkins smiled at Myrtle. "I'd be honored to pay for your lunch. What you did was very impressive, Mrs. Clover. You were just like a professional operative."

Myrtle beamed at the word *operative*.

"I only wish I could join you myself, but now my hands will be full with paperwork and questioning as we wrap things up. But I think Mr. Bradford should escort you since you've been a little unsteady. I have the feeling he's been waiting anxiously for news."

Perkins pulled his wallet out of his pocket. Myrtle's eyes lit up as Perkins handed her two twenty-dollar bills.

Red glowered at the money. "Perkins, it's just the diner. The most expensive entrée there is $8.00."

"I insist. Mrs. Clover, you put yourself in harm's way to further the course of justice. Great job."

Myrtle straightened up proudly. She thanked him for the lunch as Perkins was called away.

"Need me to give you a ride, Mama?" asked Red.

She shook her head. "I'm going to call Miles. I know he wants to be filled in."

Myrtle pulled out her phone and rang Miles. He answered the phone immediately.

"Lunch is on me," she said with a grin.

About the Author

Elizabeth writes the Southern Quilting mysteries and Memphis Barbeque mysteries for Penguin Random House and the Myrtle Clover series for Midnight Ink and independently. She blogs at ElizabethSpannCraig.com/blog, named by Writer's Digest as one of the 101 Best Websites for Writers. Elizabeth makes her home in Matthews, North Carolina, with her husband. She's the mother of two.

Sign up for Elizabeth's free newsletter to stay updated on releases:

https://bit.ly/2xZUXqO

This and That

I love hearing from my readers. You can find me on Facebook as Elizabeth Spann Craig Author, on Twitter as elizabethscraig, on my website at elizabethspanncraig.com, and by email at elizabethspanncraig@gmail.com.

Thanks so much for reading my book...I appreciate it. If you enjoyed the story, would you please leave a short review on the site where you purchased it? Just a few words would be great. Not only do I feel encouraged reading them, but they also help other readers discover my books. Thank you!

Did you know my books are available in print and ebook formats? Most of the Myrtle Clover series is available in audio and some of the Southern Quilting mysteries are. Find the audiobooks here.

Please follow me on BookBub for my reading recommendations and release notifications.

I'd also like to thank some folks who helped me put this book together. Thanks to my cover designer, Karri Klawiter, for her awesome covers. Thanks to my editor, Judy Beatty for her help. Thanks to beta readers Amanda Arrieta, Rebecca Wahr, Cassie Kelley, and Dan Harris for all of their helpful suggestions and careful reading. Thanks to my ARC readers for helping to spread the word. Thanks, as always, to my family and readers.

Other Works by Elizabeth

Myrtle Clover Series in Order (be sure to look for the Myrtle series in audio, ebook, and print):

Pretty is as Pretty Dies

Progressive Dinner Deadly

A Dyeing Shame

A Body in the Backyard

Death at a Drop-In

A Body at Book Club

Death Pays a Visit

A Body at Bunco

Murder on Opening Night

Cruising for Murder

Cooking is Murder

A Body in the Trunk

Cleaning is Murder

Edit to Death

Hushed Up

A Body in the Attic

Murder on the Ballot

Death of a Suitor

A Dash of Murder (2022)

Southern Quilting Mysteries in Order:

Quilt or Innocence

Knot What it Seams

Quilt Trip

Shear Trouble

Tying the Knot

Patch of Trouble

Fall to Pieces

Rest in Pieces

On Pins and Needles

Fit to be Tied

Embroidering the Truth

Knot a Clue

Quilt-Ridden (2021)

The Village Library Mysteries in Order (Debuting 2019):

Checked Out

Overdue

Borrowed Time

Hush-Hush

Where There's a Will (2021)

Memphis Barbeque Mysteries in Order (Written as Riley Adams):

Delicious and Suspicious

Finger Lickin' Dead

Hickory Smoked Homicide

Rubbed Out

And a standalone "cozy zombie" novel: Race to Refuge, written as Liz Craig

Printed in Great Britain
by Amazon